I look awful, Kit thought wretchedly. Just awful.

And then, as she tilted her head, she caught sight of him, the person walking behind her.

In horror she stood there, frozen, one foot lifted for the next step, her eyes staring into the other eyes reflected in the mirror.

It can't be, she told herself. There can't be anyone behind me. The hall was vacant when I came out of my room. Anyone behind me now would have had to come out of it with me, and that's impossible.

And yet the man was there, his image as clear as her own, standing so close behind her that it was incredible that she did not feel his breath upon the back of her neck.

Dragging in her breath, Kit did the only thing that she could do. She closed her eyes and screamed.

LOIS DUNCAN is the author of over thirty best-selling books for young people and adults. Her novels have won her high acclaim and many have been chosen as ALA Best Books for Young Adults and Junior Literary Guild selections. Her most recent novel for Delacorte Press was *Don't Look Behind You*. Among her most popular suspense stories for young people are *The Twisted Window, Killing Mr. Griffin, Stranger with My Face, Summer of Fear, Daughters of Eve, Locked in Time, Down a Dark Hall, Ransom,* and *The Third Eye,* all available in Dell Laurel-Leaf editions.

Lois Duncan is a full-time writer and a contributing editor to *Woman's Day* magazine. She lives with her family in Albuquerque, New Mexico.

ALSO AVAILABLE IN LAUREL-LEAF BOOKS:

DAUGHTERS OF EVE, Lois Duncan
DON'T LOOK BEHIND YOU, Lois Duncan
KILLING MR. GRIFFIN, Lois Duncan
LOCKED IN TIME, Lois Duncan
RANSOM, Lois Duncan
STRANGER WITH MY FACE, Lois Duncan
SUMMER OF FEAR, Lois Duncan
THE DARK AND DEADLY POOL, Joan Lowery Nixon
THE THIRD EYE, Lois Duncan
THE TWISTED WINDOW, Lois Duncan

Down
a
Dark
Hall

LOIS DUNCAN

Published by
Dell Publishing
a division of
Bantam Doubleday Dell Publishing Group, Inc.
1540 Broadway
New York, New York 10036

ISBN: 0-440-91805-7
RL: 6.0

Reprinted by arrangement with Little, Brown and Company,
Inc.

Printed in the United States of America.
One previous edition
October 1990

16   15   14

RAD

For Dan and Betty Sabo

Down
A
Dark
Hall

Chapter 1

———————

They had been driving since dawn, and for the past two hours, since they had turned off the highway onto the winding road that led through the hill country, Kit Gordy had been sleeping. Perhaps not completely sleeping — there had been a part of her mind that had remained awake, conscious of the curves of the road, of the faint warmth of the September sunlight slanting through the window to lie upon her hair, of the two voices in the front seat, her mother's light and lilting, Dan's low-pitched and even.

But she rode with her eyes closed and her head settled against the back of the seat. In this way she could keep from entering into the conversation.

I will not talk to them, she told herself. I have nothing to say to them.

Yet when the car drew to a stop, she could not keep herself from opening her eyes. When she did, she found her mother turned sideways, looking back at her.

"Hi, sleepyhead," she said. "You've been missing a lot of pretty countryside — pastures and brooks and rolling hills. It's been like something out of a picture book."

3

"Has it?" Kit said with disinterest. She straightened in the seat and glanced out of the window. "Are we stopping for gas?"

"That and directions," Dan Rheardon told her. "According to the map, this must be Blackwood Village, though I'm darned if I can find a sign to tell us so. It shouldn't be far to the school now. Madame Duret's letter said it was only about ten miles past the town limits."

The service station was small, with only one pump and one attendant who could be seen through the open door, sitting with his feet propped on the cash register, reading a magazine. Kit glanced down the narrow street where the one block was lined with storefronts — a grocery, a pharmacy, a hardware store, a shop with a display of dress goods in the window.

"It's the middle of nowhere," she said. "There isn't even a movie theater."

"I think it's nice," Mrs. Rheardon said. "I grew up in a little town like this one and it was delightful, with no noise, no pressure, everybody knowing everybody else. I didn't realize places like this existed anymore."

"When we get back from Europe," Dan said, "maybe we can find one. To live in, I mean." His voice was gentle — *sloshy*, Kit thought — like something from a Sunday afternoon television program. But her mother did not seem to think so, for she smiled and tilted her head, looking almost girlish, despite the lines at the corners of her eyes and the faint sheen of silver in her dark hair.

"Could we?" she asked. "But, Dan, your work —"

"They have lawyers in little towns as well as big ones. Or I could just drop law altogether and open a movie theater in Blackwood Village."

They laughed together, and Kit turned her head.

"Nowhere," she grumbled again. "A whole year here! I won't be able to stand it."

"I wouldn't worry." The gentleness was gone from Dan's voice. "I doubt that you'll be getting into the village very often. Your life will be pretty well centered around the school."

He gave the horn a beep and the attendant looked up startled, took a moment to adjust to the summons, and slowly laid his magazine on the counter. He stretched, yawned, and finally got to his feet to come begrudgingly out to the car.

"Want some gas, Mister?"

"Fill it up, please," Dan said. "Can you direct us to Blackwood School for Girls?"

"Around here?" The man looked bewildered.

"It's a boarding school run by a Madame Duret. The post office address is Blackwood Village, but the school itself is supposed to be out of town a way. It used to be a private home owned by a man named Brewer."

"Oh, the Brewer place!" The man nodded in recognition. "Well, sure, I know where that is. I did hear that some foreign lady had bought the place. She's had some of the town people up there during the summer putting it in shape, fixing the roof and the grounds and all. I think she's hired Bob Culler's girl Natalie to do kitchen work."

"Can you tell us how to get there?" Dan asked patiently.

"That's easy enough. Just follow this road through town and out the other side. It'll take you up into the hills, and you'll see a private road cutting in from the left."

The man moved to the gas pump, and Kit sighed, leaning her head back against the seat.

"Honey, please." Her mother turned to look at her with worried eyes. "Just give the school a chance. The pictures were so lovely with that marvelous old house and

5

the pond and the woods all around it, and Madame Duret was so charming when we met her last spring. You seemed happy enough about going when we first suggested it."

"That's when I thought Tracy was going," Kit said. "I still don't see why I couldn't go to Europe with you and Dan. I wouldn't be any trouble. I'm fourteen and can look after myself; it wouldn't be as though you were dragging a child around with you."

"Kit, that's enough." There was an edge to Dan's voice. "We've been over it and over it. I know your position in the family has been different from that of most girls; with just the two of you, your mother has treated you as an equal rather than as a child. You're strong-willed and independent and very used to running things. But you are *not* going along with us on our honeymoon."

"But, I don't see —" Kit began.

Dan interrupted her. "No more, now. You're upsetting your mother."

The attendant came to the car window and Dan paid him and started the engine. They pulled out onto the street and drove past the block of shopfronts and past another two blocks of small white houses, and then across a bridge over a narrow river where water swirled in frothy tumult between gray stones. Then the town was behind them and they began to climb.

Trees grew thicker along the sides of the road as the fields gave way to woodland. Dense and dark and still smelling of summer, they laced their branches across the road. Like guards, Kit thought, protecting something that lies beyond.

Growing up in the city, she had never had a chance to really know trees, only the ones in the park and the few small, thin ones in front of the public library. If you watched those carefully you could mark the seasons by

6

their leaves — translucent green ones in the springtime which drooped in the summer and crinkled and fell with the autumn frost.

The trees they passed now were different, wild and strange, living a separate life of their own. Country trees. Mountain trees.

"There's nothing lovelier than upper New York State in the autumn," Kit's mother had said when the brochure describing Blackwood had arrived in the mail. "The school sounds perfect — a small, select number of students, individual instruction in music and art, and all sorts of advanced studies that you wouldn't get in a public high school. When you graduate from Blackwood, Kit, you should be able to get into any college in the country."

"This Madame Duret has an impressive background," Dan had added, studying the written material. "She was formerly owner and headmistress of a girls' school in London and before that she had one in Paris. And she has a fantastic knowledge of art. I recall reading an article about her once in *Newsweek*. One of the paintings she picked up somewhere at an auction turned out to be an original Vermeer."

"That would interest Tracy," Kit had said. Her best friend, Tracy Rosenblum, hoped someday to become an artist.

"I wonder," her mother had said thoughtfully, "if the Rosenblums might want to consider sending Tracy to Blackwood. They can certainly afford it, and the two of you have been inseparable."

"Do you suppose they might?" Kit's enthusiasm had perked up tremendously. She and Tracy had been close friends since grammar school. Going away to boarding school wouldn't be so bad if Tracy were going also.

So for six weeks she had drifted along, accepting what came — her mother's marriage to Dan, their plan for a European honeymoon, the reams of tests that were necessary for entrance to Blackwood.

Then the notice had arrived that Tracy had not been accepted. It was as though the bottom had dropped out of Kit's world.

"I'm not going!" she had stormed. "It won't be any fun without Tracy." But for the first time in her life, she had found herself faced with a stubbornness that matched her own.

"Of course, you're going," Dan had told her firmly. "You'll make new friends. Knowing you, I won't be surprised if you're elected president of the student body the first week you get there." He had smiled when he said it but the tone of his voice had left no room for argument.

Kit had clung to one last hope that her mother might intercede for her, but that had faded today with each passing mile. Now they were on the final lap of the journey, with Blackwood only a matter of minutes away. There could be no turning back at this point; it was time to face the inevitable.

They almost missed the road because it was not paved. Dan hit the brakes, brought the car to a stop, and backed it up again.

"Do you suppose that's it?" he asked, frowning. "There isn't any name on it. You'd think there would be a sign of some sort directing us in."

"Let's give it a try," Kit's mother suggested. "We've come a good ten miles, and there haven't been any other roads."

"Nothing to lose, I guess." Dan pulled into the lane, and Kit could feel the tires sink a little in the rich, damp soil.

8

They inched their way along for several yards, and then the road curved and suddenly the trees had closed in around them. The highway behind them might never have existed, for they were in a world of cool darkness where the only sound was the rustle of leaves and the only odor the wild, sweet smell of earth and woods.

"This can't be right," Dan said.

They continued inching forward as the road twisted and rose and turned again, and suddenly they were passing through an open gate in a high spiked fence. Gravel crunched beneath the wheels.

"This is it," Kit exclaimed, startled into speech. "There's the sign — this is Blackwood!"

For a moment she forgot that she did not want to be there and simply sat, staring wide-eyed at the vista that had opened before them. There on a rise above them stood a house such as she had never envisioned in her strangest dreams.

It was huge, three stories tall with a black slate roof so steep that it seemed to fall rather than slope to its outer edge. The walls were of gray stone, no two of the same size and shape, yet arranged somehow, one upon another, so as to fit together like a child's jigsaw puzzle. The great front door was flanked by stone lions and the steps leading down to the driveway were fashioned of the same stone. Centered on the second-floor level there was a deep-set window of stained glass. The other windows were more ordinary in construction, but the late afternoon sunlight struck them now in such a way that it seemed as though the entire interior of the mansion was ablaze with orange flames.

"Good grief," Dan said slowly, letting his breath out in a low whistle. "You won't be missing a thing, Kit, by not going with us to Europe. You're going to be living in a castle the like of which you'd never see along the Rhine River."

"It couldn't have looked like this in the brochure," Kit said. "It just couldn't have."

She tried to picture the photograph of the school that had been part of the folder, but she could not see it in her mind. It seemed to her that it had been of an ordinary-enough-looking building, large, of course, as a school would have to be, but nothing to cause one to gasp and stare.

"The picture didn't do it justice," her mother said now. "And to think, this was once a private residence! It's hard to imagine what sort of people must have lived here, way up in the hills so far from the nearest little town."

Dan shifted into first gear and they continued up the driveway.

But for some reason it seemed to Kit that they were not covering any distance. The house stood above them still, no closer than it had been when they had turned in at the gate. It was an illusion, she knew, something to do with the curve of the driveway and the angle at which they were approaching, but the car itself did not seem to be moving. It was as if the house were growing larger, reaching out its great gray arms to gather them in.

She could not move her eyes from the glowing windows, dancing before her like a hundred miniature suns.

Kit shivered with the sensation of an icy wind blowing across her heart.

"Mother," she said softly, and then, more loudly, "Mom?"

"What is it, honey?" Her mother turned in the seat to look back at her.

"I don't want to stay here," Kit said.

"Now, look," Dan said impatiently, "there's no use rehashing this. We're not taking you abroad with us, and that's final. You'd better accept it, Kit. Your mother and I —"

"That's not it," Kit said frantically. "I don't care where I stay, Dan. I'll go back to the city and live with the Rosenblums while you and Mom are gone. Or I'll go to another boarding school. There must be plenty of schools that would take me."

"Whatever is wrong, darling?" her mother asked with concern. "It's a quaint-looking place, but it's really rather wonderful. You'll get used to it. Before you know it, you'll be as much at home here as you were in P.S. 37."

"I'll never be at home here!" Kit cried. "Can't you feel it, Mom? There's something about the place — something —"

She could not find the word she was seeking, and so she fell silent as the house grew nearer and nearer and then was upon them.

Dan stopped the car and got out and came around to open the doors.

"Here we are," he said. "Hop out. We may as well check in with Madame Duret, and I'll come back out for the luggage."

And then Kit knew the word for which she had been searching. The word was "evil."

Chapter 2

———◆———

The woman who answered the door was completely gray. Her hair was like gray straw, pulled back into a tight bun, and she had the sharp little eyes of a gray mouse. She wore a gray dress, hemmed low, and covered by a starched white apron.

Her eyes flicked quickly from Kit to her mother and then to Dan. For a moment Kit had the impression that she was going to close the door in their faces.

"I'm Mr. Rheardon," Dan said to block this possibility. "This is my wife and her daughter, Kathryn Gordy. Madame Duret is expecting us."

"This is Monday." The gray woman spoke with a voice so heavily accented that it was difficult to comprehend the words. "Until tomorrow the school it does not open."

"We're aware of that," Dan said. "We've made special arrangements for Kit to arrive a day early. Mrs. Rheardon and I are leaving the country tomorrow and we need to start back to the coast tonight."

"This is not the day," the woman said again. "The classes, they do not begin yet."

"Lola!" A voice spoke from the hallway beyond. "These people are expected."

A moment later the maid had moved aside and Madame Duret herself stood framed in the doorway, smiling a greeting.

She had not changed, Kit thought, in the months since they had first seen her. That had been in May when she had come into the city to give Kit and Tracy entrance examinations. She had seemed an imposing figure then, and now, against the setting of Blackwood, she was even more so.

Madame Duret was a tall woman, five foot nine or ten, with olive coloring and a striking, high-boned face. Her height was increased by a pile of rich, black hair which she wore high on her head like a crown, and the strength of her face was accentuated by black brows and a sharp, straight nose. But her most striking feature was her eyes. They were dark and deep-set with a gaze so intense that it could almost be felt physically.

"How nice it is to see you again." Madame's voice was low-pitched and gracious, with only the slightest suggestion of a French accent. "You must forgive us. Life here has been so disorganized this week with all the preparations for our influx of young people that I did not have the opportunity to mention to Lola that one of our girls would be coming early."

"I hope we're not inconveniencing you," Mrs. Rheardon said. "Our ship sails tomorrow. There was simply no way —"

"But, of course! Of course! Please come in. Did you have any trouble finding us?"

"Not really," Dan said. "We got directions from the village."

They fell into step behind Madame Duret as she moved ahead of them through a hallway with a high, arched ceiling into a pleasantly furnished room with a fireplace and a color television set.

"Please, sit down." Madame gestured them to chairs. "What may I offer you? Coffee, perhaps, or wine? What about a glass of sherry?"

"That would be great," Dan said. "Ginny?"

"Lovely," said Kit's mother. "Thank you. Really, Madame Duret, I can't get over this fantastic place. Was it actually once a private home?"

"Indeed, it was," Madame said. "Lola—" She addressed an aside to the little gray woman who had appeared silently in the doorway as though in response to a silent summons, "Please to bring three sherries and a Coke. You would like a soft drink, Kathryn, would you not?"

"Yes, please," Kit said.

"This entire estate," Madame continued, turning back to the Rheardons, "was owned by a man named Brewer who died over ten years ago. Since that time it has stood vacant. The heirs, distant cousins of some kind, live on the West Coast and placed it in the hands of a realtor. No one has wanted to buy it, which is understandable; it is no normal one-family residence, as you can see, and standing empty all that time it picked up something of an unusual reputation. Teenagers from the village used to come up here to park on dates and they would go home with all sorts of weird stories about lights in the windows and bodiless creatures floating through the garden."

She laughed, and the Rheardons laughed with her.

"It sounds exciting," Kit's mother said. "I'm going to expect marvelous letters from my daughter telling us about the adventures she has here."

There was a break in the conversation as Lola came in with a tray. Kit took her glass, glad of something to hold in her hands. The dreadful feeling that had come upon

14

her at her first glimpse of Blackwood had somewhat faded, but the shadow of it still remained.

"How many students are there going to be?" she asked.

"That is never a certainty," Madame Duret told her. "There are always first-day dropouts who get homesick at the thought of leaving their parents. We'll know the final count at Orientation tomorrow. Personally, I think that going away to school is an educational experience that should be part of the life of every young woman."

The conversation continued, and Kit sat, sipping her Coke, only half listening. Tomorrow, she thought, there would be other girls in this room, laughing and chatting and tuning in favorite programs on the giant television. Perhaps, with young voices ringing through the halls, the atmosphere at Blackwood would be different. Maybe, as Dan had suggested, there would be someone among the new arrivals who would be the same kind of friend as Tracy, close and companionable and always ready to share a good time.

Dan glanced at his watch. "I hate to rush things, but we have a long drive ahead of us. I'd better go out and bring in Kit's suitcases."

"Lola will show you where to bring them." Madame Duret rose from her chair. "While you are getting the luggage, perhaps Mrs. Rheardon would enjoy a quick look at Blackwood."

"I'd love it," Kit's mother told her. "This is a fascinating old mansion. Did you have to do a great deal of renovating?"

"Not as much as one might suppose," Madame said, leading the way out into the hall. "The original building was well constructed. The only actual rebuilding that had to be done was in the upstairs dormitory wing where there had once been a fire. The stone structure withstood it well, but the wooden paneling was burned away and the furniture had to be replaced. I tried as well as I could to duplicate the style of the original pieces."

As she led the way down the hall, she gestured to various doorways, some closed, some open.

"The room we just left is the living room or, as I prefer to call it, the parlor. This door to my right leads to my office and beyond that lies a suite of rooms which I share with my son Jules. There is a guest residence out behind which has been converted to apartments for the other members of the faculty.

"Here is the dining room, and on the far side of that is the kitchen. These doors lead to classrooms."

She paused at one door, opened it, and flicked on the light. A baby grand piano took up one whole corner of the room, while along the far wall there stood an array of musical instruments. Music racks, comfortable chairs, and a large and intricate-looking tape recorder completed the furnishings.

"This, of course, is the music room," Madame Duret said. "Are you musically inclined, Kathryn?"

"I had a year of piano," Kit said, "back when I was eleven. I can't say I did too well at it."

"You just got impatient," her mother said. "You didn't want to take the time to practice. I hope that here at Blackwood you'll take advantage of the chance to get some musical training. It's something that will give you pleasure all your life."

"We devote much time and effort to the study of the arts," Madame told them, turning off the light and drawing the door closed. "If you had more time you would enjoy browsing through the library, and the paintings throughout the house represent a hobby of mine, collecting little-known works of famous artists. But I know that

16

what you are most interested to see is where it is that Kathryn herself will be living."

The stairway was curved and at its head an immense mirror seemed to double the length of the upstairs hallway. At the hall's end was the stained-glass window that had been evident from the driveway, and the sun slanted through it, lighting the hallway in rainbow hues.

A series of doors opened onto the hall from both sides. Madame Duret stopped in front of one of these, fumbled in her skirt pocket for a key, and inserted it in the brass lock. She turned it, withdrew it, and handed the key to Kit.

"We believe in privacy at Blackwood," she said. "Each student carries her own room-key and is encouraged to keep her room locked when she is not in it. And here, Kathryn, is where you will be making your nest."

She pushed the door open, and Kit heard her mother catch her breath. She herself could not contain a small gasp of surprise, for the room was far more elaborate than anything she could have imagined.

The largest piece of furniture was a bed of carved dark wood with a high, rich canopy of red velvet. Beside it sat a small table bearing an ornate lamp with a ruffled shade. Heavy gold draperies bordered a window and against the wall opposite there stood a walnut bureau, over which hung an oval mirror with a gilded frame. A Persian carpet covered the floor, and under the window there stood a rolltop desk with a study lamp.

"If this is a dorm room," Mrs. Rheardon exclaimed, "it's the kind I never dreamed of when I was a schoolgirl!"

"It's beautiful," Kit agreed, stunned in spite of herself. Tentatively she reached out and let her hand caress the bedspread. "Is this real velvet?"

17

"It is, indeed," Madame Duret told her. "We want Blackwood to be more than just a school for our students; we want it to be an experience they will carry with them long after they have left its halls. We feel that beauty enriches the spirit and that young people should learn to be at ease with lovely things."

"But there's just one bed." The thought occurred to Kit suddenly. "Won't I be having a roommate?"

"Not at Blackwood," Madame said. "All our girls have private rooms and baths. I think that privacy makes for better study habits, don't you?"

"I guess so," Kit said, recalling the plans she and Tracy had made to room together. It was true that they would probably have done more talking than studying, but it would have been fun.

"Hello, there!" Dan's voice called from the top of the stairs. "I've got a couple of bags here that feel as though they must be stuffed with bricks. Where do you want them?"

"Down here, dear," Kit's mother called back. "Come and see Kit's room. You won't believe it!"

"Good grief!" Dan appeared in the doorway, a suitcase in each hand. "This looks more like a palace than a school. You won't be able to toss your stuff all over the place here, Kit."

"We trust our girls to take care of their rooms," Madame Duret said easily. "And now, if you will excuse me, I must go down and speak to our kitchen help about dinner. We dine fairly early, Kathryn, because the girl who does the cooking lives in the village and has to drive home every evening. Dinner will be served at six-thirty in the dining room."

"Okay," Kit said. "Thank you."

"Thank you, Madame Duret," Kit's mother said. "We'll stop and say good-bye before we leave."

They all stood quiet, listening to her quick, strong footsteps as the headmistress hurried off down the hall.

"Quite a woman," Dan commented in a low voice. "Imagine what a job it must have been to turn this ancient place into a modern school."

"I'm certainly impressed." Kit's mother turned to her. "Honey —" And then suddenly she pulled her daughter to her, and Kit could hear the note of pleading in her voice. "Kit, dear, you will be happy here, won't you? I'd never enjoy a moment of our trip if I thought you weren't. We *can* make other arrangements, even if it means taking another ship later. Your happiness is the most important thing."

At that moment, Kit felt her resentment leave her. She had won, and she could not take advantage of the winning. Putting her arms around her mother, she gave her a warm hug.

"Of course, I'll like it," she said thickly. "You and Dan have a wonderful honeymoon. You deserve it, Mom, if anybody ever did. I'm sorry I've been such a pill. I'll be happy here — I promise."

There had been a question nagging at the back of her mind. It slid away now and was forgotten. It did not really matter why her bedroom at Blackwood had a lock on the outside — but not on the inside — of its door.

Chapter 3

The bed was high and beautiful, but not particularly comfortable. Kit lay back upon the velvet bedspread and stared up at the wine-colored canopy. Somebody — was it Poe? — had written a story about a bed exactly like this one in which the canopy had sunk slowly at night to smother the person unlucky enough to be sleeping beneath it. They had read it last year in literature class and there had been a barrage of squeals and laughter.

Now the story didn't seem so funny.

I don't like canopies, Kit decided, and I don't like hard mattresses. But I am going to like it at Blackwood if it kills me. I gave Mom my promise.

Her mother and Dan had been gone for over an hour now, and still she had not begun to unpack her suitcases. She had climbed onto the bed at first simply to see what it felt like and, once there, she had remained, staring up at the canopy and thinking.

She *had* been a pill over the past weeks. She could admit it now, and she was ashamed of herself. Her mother had been through enough in the way of hard work and loneliness since the death of Kit's father to deserve any happiness that fell her way. Maybe Dan wasn't the person Kit herself would have gone out and selected for a stepfather, but if her mother loved him, that was all that mattered. In all fairness, no one whom her mother chose as a second husband would have pleased Kit completely. She had been close to her father and to her no one would ever take his place.

She had been the last one to see him. No one had ever believed that, but it was true. She had been seven at the time and had awakened in the night to find her father standing at the foot of her bed, gazing down at her. Although the room had been dark, she had been able to see him clearly, his head bent, his gray eyes wistful, and a world of love reflected in his square, strong-featured face.

Kit had drawn herself up upon her elbows and stared at him.

"Dad?" she had said. "What are you doing here? I thought you were in Chicago on business."

When he had not answered she had shivered, realizing suddenly how cold the room had become even though it was midsummer. She had lain back upon the pillow, pulling the sheet and spread up to her chin, and had let her eyes close for a moment. When she had opened them again it was morning, and sunlight streamed through the windows, falling in bright golden patterns upon the bedroom rug.

She had gotten up and dressed in shorts and a T-shirt and gone downstairs. The house had been filled with people.

One of her aunts had come over and put an arm around her and said, "Poor baby! Poor little love!"

"What is it?" Kit had asked. "What's happened?" Her eyes had taken in the group before her. "Why is Mom crying?"

"It's your father, dear," her aunt had told her. "There was an accident last night and your mother only got the call about it this morning. Your father was in a taxi headed back to his hotel, when the driver went through a stop sign —"

"But that can't be true," Kit had interrupted in bewilderment. "He was here last night. I saw him. He came into my bedroom."

"You were dreaming, dear," her aunt told her gently.

"I wasn't," Kit had insisted. "I was awake. Dad was here. I saw him." Across the room she had cried to her mother, "Daddy did come home last night, didn't he? You must have gone to pick him up at the airport. Mom —"

Her mother's face had been white and terrible in grief, but she had come quickly and taken Kit in her arms.

"I wish he had, honey," she had said in a choking voice. "If only he had."

The year that followed had seen many changes in their lives. Her mother, who had never worked before, had taken a course in business school and found a secretarial job with a law firm. She had sold the house — "The payments are too high for me to manage," she had said, "and I can't keep up the yard by myself" — and had rented an apartment in the city close to the office where she worked.

Kit knew it had not been easy. Her mother was a pretty, vivacious woman, and much as she loved her daughter, there was bound to be a void in her life, a terrible longing for adult companionship. This had been proven by the change in her spirits since she had found Dan.

Mom's happy now, and I must be also, Kit told herself determinedly. If I'm not, I'll put a damper on everything.

But she could not forget that feeling in the driveway, the sudden sense of evil chill as though a cloud had slid across the sun.

If Tracy were here, they would have laughed about it. They would even have made a joke of the crimson canopy; Tracy would probably have suggested attaching bells to it so that the tinkle would wake them when it descended in the night. Tracy Rosenblum was level-headed and bright and funny, and the possibility that she might not be accepted at Blackwood had never occurred to either of them.

When the notice arrived, Kit had not been able to believe it.

"But you're an honor student!" she had exclaimed incredulously. "You always get better grades than I do!"

"Maybe it was the psychological tests," Tracy had said. "Or the interview. It's possible the woman just didn't like me."

"That's ridiculous. Everybody likes you. Besides, you knew all about her art collection and you could talk to her about the Vermeer she discovered, and she kept calling you 'chérie' with every other breath. She liked you better than she did me."

"Well, you come up with a reason then." Tracy had shrugged her shoulders philosophically. "I just didn't make it, and that's that. So back I go to old P.S. 37, and off you go to Blackwood, and it's a good thing you're good at composition because I'm going to expect a lot of letters."

"You'll get them," Kit had promised. "But there's still a chance I can talk Mom out of sending me."

Well, that chance was gone. Here she was, stretched out on velvet, staring up at more velvet, watching the room grow dim as dusk settled outside the window. I should unpack, she thought, but she made no move to do so; she felt lulled and heavy, weighted down with a strange weariness which she could not explain.

There was a rap on the door. A voice said, "Miss Kathryn?"

"Yes?" Kit came to life with a start. Guiltily she shoved her feet over the edge of the bed so that her shoes were no longer in touch with the spread. "Yes — what is it?"

"Dinner, miss." The voice was unmistakably Lola's. "The others are already down."

"Oh, thanks. I guess I lost track of time." Pushing her legs the rest of the way over the edge of the bed, Kit sat up. To her surprise she saw that in only a moment's time the twilight outside had deepened into night. The room was very dark.

Reaching over, she fumbled with the lamp on the bedside table, found a knob at its base, and turned it. The light went on and shadows leapt high against the opposite wall.

I wish there was an overhead, Kit thought, getting to her feet. There's such a thing as being too old-fashioned and charming.

She crossed to the desk and turned on the study lamp, which helped slightly. She knew she should change from her travel-wrinkled clothes, but with dinner already waiting, it seemed better not to take the time. She compromised by scrubbing her hands and face and running a comb through her thick mane of blond hair.

The face that looked back at her from the bathroom mirror was not conventionally pretty. The mouth was a little too wide, the chin too square. But the gray eyes were direct and friendly and the cheeks flushed with the glow of vitality and good health. It was a likable face, and the only time Kit really thought about it was when she saw its growing resemblance to her father's.

Leaving the lights burning in the bedroom, she stepped out into the hall and drew the door closed behind her.

Immediately she found herself standing in a tunnel of

darkness. The hall was unlighted except for a single bulb encased in a frosted globe at the top of the stairwell. Kit began to walk slowly toward it, and to her astonishment, she saw a slim, pale figure moving toward her as though out of the wall beyond the stairs.

She stopped, and the figure stopped. She took one tentative step, and realized suddenly that she was seeing her own reflection in the mirror beyond the stairs.

"I'm a great one," she said aloud, disgusted with herself. "Next thing you know I'll be seeing goblins."

Placing her hand on the smooth mahogany banister, she descended the stairs to the hall below. This was well lighted, and though it was empty she could hear the sound of voices and the clink of glasses and silverware in a room beyond. Following the sounds, she made her way down the hall to the door of the dining room and looked inside.

The room was massive with high, arched ceilings and a crystal chandelier of such grandeur that it might have been stolen from the set of a period movie. Beneath it stood a large, circular table covered with a white linen cloth and set with candles and china. Three people were seated around it, and there was a fourth place setting.

Madame Duret glanced up from the conversation to see Kit standing in the doorway.

"Come in, my dear. Forgive us for starting without you, but dinner at Blackwood is served promptly at six-thirty."

"I'm sorry," Kit said contritely. "I think I must have fallen asleep."

As she entered the room the two men at the table rose to their feet and Madame made the introductions.

"Kathryn Gordy, may I present Professor Farley and my son, Jules."

"How do you do," Kit said.

The elderly gentleman across from her had a receding hairline and a short, white beard, trimmed into a point. Kit shook his hand politely, but her eyes had already shifted past him to Jules Duret.

Slim and fine-boned, with glossy black hair which framed a face so perfect in feature that it might have belonged to a television star, he was without doubt the handsomest young man she had ever seen.

"Won't you sit down?" Madame Duret asked pleasantly. She reached over and lifted the little silver bell which stood by her water glass.

At the tinkle, a swinging door in the back of the room opened and a plain, flat-faced girl in a blue uniform appeared.

"Miss Kathryn is here now, Natalie," Madame said. "She will have her soup." She smiled at Kit as she took her place at the table. "It is pleasant to have you with us a day early, Kathryn. Professor Farley will be your instructor in math and sciences. Jules has just received his degree from a music conservatory in England and will be teaching piano."

"Are the other teachers not here yet?" Kit asked, unfolding her napkin and placing it in her lap.

There was a slight pause.

"There are not to be any others," Jules said. His voice had the same charming blend of accents as his mother's, so subtle as to be almost undetectable, yet adding a note of color to his speech.

Kit regarded him with surprise. "You're kidding, aren't you?"

"I, too, will be teaching," Madame told her. "I will instruct in languages and literature, and, of course, in art, if there should be an interest."

"But the brochure said 'small classes,'" Kit exclaimed. "How can they be with only three people to teach them?"

"You mustn't worry about that, Kathryn." Professor Farley's wise old eyes seemed to twinkle in the candlelight. "You will receive all the personal attention at Blackwood that you could possibly ask for. I had the pleasure of visiting Madame Duret's school in England several years ago and was so impressed by her achievements there that I convinced her to open a school here in the United States."

"How is your room, chérie?" Madame asked. "There is a supply of extra blankets if you need them. Are there enough hangers in the closet?"

"Everything seems fine," Kit said. She hesitated and then added, "There's one thing — the light in the hall seems awfully dim. I didn't notice it this afternoon because of the light from the window, but now at night it's really pretty black."

"That's one of the problems that comes with renovating an old place," Professor Farley said. "That upstairs wiring just doesn't do the trick. Madame has been trying to get electricians out from the village, but that's easier said than done."

"Perhaps we could remove the globe," Madame Duret said, "and use a bulb of a higher wattage. As a temporary measure, of course, until we can have another fixture installed."

"Oh, that's all right," Kit said in sudden embarrassment. "I didn't mean to make a big deal out of it. I'm not usually worried about things like that, it's just that the dorm floor is so empty right now. It won't matter at all tomorrow when the other girls get here and it's all filled up with people."

There was a moment's silence. Madame Duret lifted her napkin to dab at her lips. Professor Farley took a sip from his water glass.

Kit turned to Jules, whose head was bent over his plate.

"It will be different tomorrow," she said again, "after everybody gets here."

"Naturally," Jules said. "It will seem different then." He lifted his head, but his eyes did not meet hers, and there was a strange, closed-in look on his face.

She dreamed that the canopy was lowering. Twice she dreamed it. Slowly, softly, the air was pressing down upon her as the great, billowing bubble of wine-colored velvet descended to settle over her face.

The first time she woke, shaking, she groped frantically for the lamp on the bedside table. She pressed the button at its base, and at once the room was filled with dim, yellow light.

Sitting up, Kit stared about her at the room. It lay in perfect order except for a pile of her own clothing which she had tossed in her usual careless manner onto a chair, and the two suitcases, still only partially unpacked, which lay open on the floor before the closet.

The canopy stood high above her, just where it should have been.

Kit turned off the light and lay back upon the pillow, and after a bit she slept. When she woke again, from the same dream, she turned the lamp on and left it burning for the rest of the night.

Chapter 4

------◆------

When she awoke in the morning, Kit could laugh at herself for her midnight foolishness. Bright sunshine poured in the window, falling in golden splashes across the rich hues of the carpet and picking up the gleam of the woodwork in a way that made the room seem aglow with beauty. The canopy was only a canopy, a regal decoration for what must undoubtedly be classed as one of the world's most elegant beds.

Kit swung her legs over the side and placed her bare feet on the rug. It felt thick and luxurious, and she dug her toes into it as she crossed the room to the window. Once there, she wondered how she could possibly not have looked out of it before, for the view was so spectacular that her heart leapt with pleasure.

Below her lay a garden, still partially abloom with late summer flowers, and through it ran a narrow, gravel walkway which wound about like a maze, splitting and turning and meeting itself once again. Beyond this lay a stretch of lawn that led down to a pond. The pond was not large, but it shimmered like silver in the morning light, smooth and flat and luminous as a mirror. Past that

rose the woods, circling protectively around the opposite shore and coming in a full curve to border Blackwood on all sides.

Above everything rose the sky, blue and clear in a high,
rich arc. The air smelled fresh and sweet.

From this side of the house, Kit was not able to catch
sight of the driveway. She could imagine it filled with
cars from which harried fathers were busily extracting
suitcases. In a short time now there would be other girls
rollicking about the hall, laughing and chattering, com-
paring backgrounds and rushing inquisitively in and out
of each other's rooms.

I'm just as glad I got here early, Kit thought as she
dressed. This way I have sort of a head start.

She made her bed and unpacked her suitcases, hanging
the dresses in the closet and folding other clothing to
place in bureau drawers. In the second suitcase she had
packed her photographs. One was of Tracy and herself,
taken three years before at Tracy's eleventh birthday
party. They were giggling and posing self-consciously
with their arms around each other's shoulders and a
mammoth cake in front of them.

The other picture was of her parents on their honeymoon. Her mother had had it enlarged and framed for
her soon after her father's death.

"I want you to remember him," she had said.

As though I could ever *not* remember, Kit thought
now, studying the picture. Her father's clear eyes laughed
out at her and the stubborn chin, so much like her own,
gave a look of strength to a face still curved and boyish.
The girl clinging to his arm was harder to remember. Had
her mother ever really been that young and carefree, so
radiant with joy?

Be happy, Mom, Kit told her silently. Please, be happy

with Dan. For no matter what companionship and security her mother found in her second marriage, Kit knew in her heart that she would never again be the girl in this picture.

She set the photograph of her parents on the bureau and tucked the snapshot of herself and Tracy into the rim of the mirror. Why, she wondered, hadn't she brought any pictures of boys? She had a batch of them at home, for last spring everybody had traded class pictures, and a mass of snapshots had been taken at parties. From what she had heard they were standard decorations for dorm rooms.

Oh, well, Kit thought resignedly, any specimens I could have come up with would have looked pretty scroungy with Jules Duret for contrast. I bet Blackwood turns out to have a lot of dedicated piano students.

Yesterday's doldrums were over. Today the world was bright and shining. When she left the room she found the hallway flooded with rainbow light as it had been the afternoon before. The figure approaching from the depths of the mirror did not startle her now; instead she looked like a friend. Kit waved and smiled at her, pleased with the neat, bright-faced image who waved back.

There was no one in the downstairs hall, but a murmur of voices came from behind the closed door of Madame's office. Kit swung on past it and into the dining room, and found it empty. The rattle of pans and the sound of running water came to her from the room beyond. Crossing through the dining room, Kit pushed open the swinging door and entered the kitchen.

The thin girl who had served dinner the night before was standing at the sink, washing dishes. She glanced up and frowned as Kit came in.

"Breakfast is over, miss, but the lady says I'm to fix you

something if you want it. They had their breakfasts at eight o'clock. It's past ten now."

"I slept late," Kit said apologetically, "and then I unpacked. My name's Kit Gordy. You're Natalie, aren't you?"

The girl nodded. "Natalie Culler. What do you want to eat?"

"Don't worry about fixing me breakfast," Kit said. "I'll just make myself some toast if that's okay."

The girl made a gesture to forestall her.

"That's my job. I do the cooking." She removed two slices of bread from a wrapped loaf and placed them in the toaster. "After all, it's what I'm getting paid for."

"You wait table and do the cooking too?" Kit exclaimed. "That's an awfully big job for one person. Will there be somebody to help you when all the students get here?"

"There won't be that many," Natalie said. "I'm eighteen now and I've done cooking off and on since I was twelve. A few extra don't make much difference."

"But, gosh — a whole school full of girls!" Kit regarded her with awe. "Won't that mean —"

The girl interrupted. "Your toast's up, miss. Here's the butter, and there's jam over there on the counter." She paused and then added in a more friendly manner, "The lady — Madame Duret — she doesn't want the village help talking with the students. She told us all that when she hired us. I can ask people what they want and things like that, but that's all the talking I'm supposed to do."

"Oh," Kit said awkwardly. "Well, I didn't mean to do anything to get you in trouble."

"I know that, miss, but this job means a lot to me. Full-time work isn't easy to find in a place like Blackwood Village. So maybe it's best you take your breakfast and go eat it in the dining room, all right?"

"Okay," Kit said. "Sure."

She pushed open the kitchen door and went through into the room beyond. The door swung closed behind her, shutting off the everyday world of the kitchen area, and immediately the dark beauty of the Blackwood dining room surrounded her. The room's floor-level windows were shielded from the outside by shrubbery so that the light that did slip through between the leaves was dim and diffused. The round table glowed gently with polish and the crystal chandelier hung silent and pale above it.

The room was so empty, so devoid of movement or sound, that Kit hurried through it without being tempted to sit down and went out once again into the entrance hall.

The door to the office stood open now. Madame stood just inside, talking to a slight, red-haired girl.

She turned as Kit came opposite the doorway and said, "Here is one of our students now. Kathryn, come here, dear. I want you to meet Sandra Mason."

"Hello," Kit said, pleased to see a young face.

"Hi." The bright-haired girl smiled shyly. She had a narrow, elfin face and an uptilted nose that was sprinkled with freckles.

"Sandra came by bus as far as the village," Madame Duret explained, "and Professor Farley met her there and drove her the rest of the way to Blackwood. Would you show her upstairs, Kathryn? Her room will be 211, the corner room at the end of the hall."

"I'll be glad to," Kit said, suddenly feeling ridiculous with her hands full of toast. She glanced about for a place to deposit it, saw none, and decided to make the best of the situation. "Would you like some breakfast?"

"No, thank you," the girl said seriously. "I ate in the village." A few moments later, as they mounted the stairs, she said, "I didn't really."

"Didn't really what?" Kit asked.

"I ordered some coffee and a doughnut at a drugstore, but I couldn't eat them. I guess I was too excited. You see, I've never been away to school before."

"Neither have I," Kit told her. "I got here yesterday, and I wasn't exactly prepared for what it would be like."

"The house waiting at the end of the drive — when I saw it from the car I couldn't believe it —"

"If you think that was something," Kit said, "wait until you see the bedrooms."

Room 211 was identical to Kit's, except that it was a corner room with one window facing the driveway. It was done in greens and golds instead of red, but the ornate furnishings, the plush carpet and the heavy draperies were the same.

Kit could see on Sandra's face the same amazement that she herself had experienced the day before.

"It's so — different!" the girl exclaimed. "I guess I should have realized from the brochure, but somehow it just didn't come across as — as quite like this."

"It sure didn't," Kit agreed. "It's like living in a palace. I was the only one sleeping on the hall last night, and I kept having funny dreams. I hope they don't come with the bedrooms as built-in accessories."

"I hope not too. I'm not exactly the world's soundest sleeper." The girl smiled nervously. "By the way, I go by 'Sandy.' I can't remember anyone's ever calling me 'Sandra' except Madame Duret."

"And I'm never 'Kathryn,' " Kit said. "I'm 'Kit.' Do you know what's funny? The morning's almost over and I haven't seen anybody but you. Wouldn't you think that a lot of the students would have gotten here by this time?"

"Someone's arriving now," Sandy said. "I can hear a

car in the driveway." She crossed to the window and stood, looking out. "There are two girls and a man. He must be the chauffeur; he's wearing a uniform."

"But no parents?" Kit went over to stand beside her. "That seems funny, doesn't it? You'd think any parents would want to see their daughters get settled and take a look at where they'll be living." She caught herself and grew red with embarrassment. "I'm sorry. I wasn't thinking."

"That's all right," Sandy said. "My family would have liked to have brought me but they don't drive. I live with my grandparents. They're moving into a retirement village that doesn't take teenagers, and it seemed as though it would be best for me to come away to school and just visit them on vacations."

"My mother just got married," Kit said, feeling she had to volunteer something or seem unfriendly. "She and my stepfather are honeymooning in Europe." She leaned forward, studying the two girls who had climbed from the car and were watching the chauffeur unload their belongings. "That blond's pretty, isn't she? I bet she hooks Jules right out from under our noses."

"Jules?" Sandy said blankly.

"Madame Duret's son. Young, dark and handsome — a real dream guy. He's going to be our music instructor."

"That sounds like a challenge for somebody," Sandy said. "Did you date much back home?"

"A fair amount. I didn't leave a steady or anything if that's what you mean. How about you?"

"My grandparents are old-fashioned. They don't think a girl should go out until she's old enough to get married." Sandy sighed. "Not that it mattered. Nobody's ever asked me."

"They will," Kit said comfortingly.

"I suppose." Sandy turned away from the window and went to open the door to the hall.

A few moments later they could hear the clatter of footsteps on the stairs and the sound of excited voices. Lola's expressionless voice was saying, "Rooms 208 and 206, on your left, ladies."

"What a funny hall! The window at the end makes it all different colors!" The high, light voice of the blond girl rose liltingly as she hurried ahead of her companions.

"Why, hi!" she said as she saw Kit and Sandy. "I'm glad somebody's here! I was beginning to think we'd come on the wrong day!"

"We're glad to see you too," Kit told her. "I'm Kit Gordy and this is Sandy Mason."

"I'm Lynda Hannah," the girl said, "and this is Ruth Stark. We're both old hands at boarding schools but, I swear, I've never seen one like this!" Her exquisite, china-doll face was bright with excitement, and the pale hair framed it like a halo.

Her friend was a complete contrast, a short, heavy-set girl with a smooth, dark cap of hair and a downy shadow across her upper lip. Her thick brows met each other across the bridge of her nose, and her eyes were sharp and alert behind wire-rimmed glasses.

She acknowledged Kit's greeting with a nod and turned to open the door of her room.

"Cripes!" she exclaimed as the interior became visible to her. "Will you look at that, Lynda!"

"Oh, let me see mine!" the blond girl gasped. "I wonder if it's the same!" She hurried down the hall to the next door.

"Come on," Kit said to Sandy. "Let's look out and see who's coming next."

They reentered Sandy's room and crossed to the window. The driveway below was empty. Even the chauffeured car that had brought Lynda and Ruth had disappeared. The drive stretched flat and straight, bordered by shrubbery, down to the black iron fence, and beyond that the trees crowded close like a line of sentinels. The sun was high in the sky and threw no shadows.

"I guess it'll be a real mob scene this afternoon," said Sandy. "The people who plan to drive up in one day won't be coming till later. I wonder, though, why there weren't any other students on the bus this morning. After all, there can't be many buses coming through a little place like Blackwood Village."

"It does seem strange," Kit said. She gazed out past the driveway to the fence. Something was different. Something had changed since the last time she had looked through this window.

"Sandy," she said slowly, "I — I think — there aren't going to be any other students."

"No more students?" Her new friend turned to her incredulously. "You've got to be kidding. *Four* students in this great huge place? That's ridiculous!"

"Ridiculous or not," Kit said, "I don't think they're expecting anybody else. The gate at the end of the driveway has been closed."

"Yes, it is true. We have only accepted four students for our first session." Madame Duret smiled at them across the dining table. The candles flickered above the white cloth, and an unfelt breeze seemed to touch the crystals of the chandelier, moving them against each other with a faint tinkle as of distant music.

They had just completed the soup course, and Natalie had not come in yet to clear the table.

"There were many applicants," Professor Farley inter-

37

jected. "The problem was that most of them didn't fill our requirements."

"You mean they couldn't pass the tests?" Kit asked in bewilderment. "I don't understand. The examinations weren't that hard. *I* passed them, and I'm not an all-A student."

"None of you are, except for Ruth." Professor Farley nodded toward the dark-haired girl, who reacted with a little smile of satisfaction. "Your selection was not based entirely upon your academic accomplishments. There were other considerations."

"Like what?" Lynda Hannah asked. "Like who our parents are?"

"It can't be that," Sandy said softly from her seat on Kit's right. "I don't have parents."

"Let us just say that we found you four very special girls." Madame's eyes were like mirrors, reflecting the glow of the candles. When Kit leaned forward, she could see her own image peering back at her from the luminous pupils. "You have just the attributes we want our students to possess. Does it displease you to be part of a small class?"

"I like the idea," Ruth said in her clipped, no-nonsense way. "This way we'll get individual attention and advance faster. That's the whole reason I'm here. I was bored to death in the last school I attended."

"I don't know," Lynda said hesitantly. "I kind of wish there were more people. I mean, what kind of social affairs will we be having with so few of us? We can't have dances or get together with boys' schools for parties."

"You will not be bored at Blackwood. I can assure you of that." Madame lifted the little silver bell and shook it.

Immediately the kitchen door opened and Natalie came in.

"We are ready for the main course," Madame told her.

Kit was seated directly across from Jules Duret. How much, she found herself wondering, did he have to do with the selection of the students?

She glanced over and flushed to find him studying her. He did not shift his gaze when their eyes met, but continued looking at her, as though trying to fathom some part of her that did not show upon the surface.

"My mother is right," he said slowly. "You will not be bored."

Chapter 5

———◆———

It was twelve-thirty — half past midnight — on the eighth day of September, and Kit lay sprawled across the bed, writing a letter to Tracy. She knew it was late to be writing letters. If she had been at home with her light on at this hour her mother would have been rapping at the door, calling in a worried voice, "Kit? Is anything wrong, honey? It's much too late for you to be up."

At Blackwood nobody sounded a lights-off curfew, and Kit was glad. Although she had been at the school for well over a week now and was adjusting well on most counts, she still did not feel at ease at night. The light at the end of the hall had not been fixed — "It's almost impossible to get electricians to come out this far," Madame explained apologetically — and though Kit's own room was often lightened by moonlight, she could not shut out a strange nervousness about the oppressive darkness on the far side of her closed door.

She did not sleep well at Blackwood. She dreamed. She knew that she dreamed, for when she woke in the mornings the feeling of the dreams still clung to the edges of her mind, and yet in most cases she could not remember

40

what they had been. She needed to be very sleepy to turn off the light and settle into slumber, and so she had begun to form the habit of studying and writing letters during the early part of the night.

"Dear Tracy," she wrote now, "I'm sorry to have been so long in writing. I got a note off to Mom the first day here so that she would have mail waiting for her in Cherbourg, and then I got snowed under with schoolwork. The work here is harder than it was in public school, mostly, I guess, because the classes are so small. There are only four of us here — can you believe it? Four students in the entire school! So it's almost like having private tutors. I'm taking math and science from Professor Farley, a dear old goat of a man with a funny little beard — really sweet — and literature from Madame Duret. And piano from *Jules!* I guess I'd better put a row of exclamation marks — !!!!!!!! — to give you an idea of what *he* looks like. All of a sudden I'm getting interested in music.

"The three other girls here are very different. My favorite is Sandy Mason — she's shy and quiet, but nice, and I've started to stir her up a little with plans to short-sheet the other girls' beds and maybe raid the kitchen one night and bring the food up to the rooms for a midnight feast. Lynda Hannah and Ruth Stark knew each other before. They went to the same prep school last year, and when Ruth's parents decided to switch her to Blackwood, Lynda persuaded her mother to let her change schools too. Ruth is homely but very bright, and Lynda is the opposite, awfully pretty but not much in the brains department. They seem to balance each other.

"I still don't understand how we four were selected. Professor Farley says we have the special attributes they were looking for in their students, but I can't imagine

41

what they might be. We seem to have nothing in common with each other, and I don't see how you could have failed to get accepted if I was. I tried to ask Madame Duret about it, but she only said that she didn't discuss test results.

"I wish I could say I like it here. In a way I do. Everybody's very nice to me, and the classes are interesting. But there's something — I don't know how to put it into words, and you'd probably laugh if I did — but I've got this creepy feeling that something's wrong. I felt it first when we entered the gates and started up the driveway, and I feel it more and more every day, as though —"

Somebody screamed. Somewhere in the blackness on the far side of the door. It was a funny scream, choked off in an instant as though a hand had been pressed suddenly to cover the mouth.

It went through Kit like an electric shock. Her hand jerked, and the pen made a lurch across the page, so that the word "though" ran off the side of the paper.

Pulling herself upright on the bed, she sat, tense and shaken, listening. There was nothing but silence.

But I heard it, she told herself. I know I heard it.

Somewhere in the quiet dormitory someone had shrieked. In pain? In terror? Perhaps only from a nightmare, and yet, perhaps for some other reason. For — *help*?

I won't, Kit thought. I can't. I just can't open that door and go out there.

And yet, what if one of the other girls were ill? No one screamed without reason. Was someone lying even now in one of the rooms along the hall, wretched with fear or in physical agony, praying that her cry had been heard and would be answered?

Slowly, as though impelled by something other than her own will, Kit got off the bed and crossed the room and opened the door. The terrible blackness of the hall stretched before her, lessened only by the patch of lamplight that fell from her own doorway. Beyond this there was nothing but stillness and dark.

Kit stood with one hand on the door jamb, listening. The only sounds she could hear were the thud of her own heart and the quick, sharp noise of her breathing.

Perhaps I imagined it, she thought. Perhaps I dozed off a little, there on the bed, and dreamed.

And then she heard it — not a scream this time but a little moaning sound, half a sob, half a wail. It seemed to come from the end of the hall where Sandy had her room.

Well, that does it, Kit told herself resignedly. I have to go.

Drawing a deep breath as if in readiness for a dive into icy water, she stood poised for a moment on the edge of the patch of light. Then, bracing herself, she stepped out into the darkness.

For an instant she felt that she actually had plunged into water. The dark rose about her, filling her eyes and nose and ears, pressing on all sides so that she could not catch her breath. As her initial panic began to subside, she forced herself to fill her chest with air. Stretching out one hand, she groped for the wall. She found it and steadied herself against it and then, carefully, one step at a time, she began to work her way down the hall toward Sandy's room.

With each step she tested the floor ahead of her. It was ridiculous, she knew, and yet the darkness was so total that it seemed that she was moving forward into nothingness, that suddenly the boards of the floor might be gone as though they had never existed and she would find herself stepping off into infinite space. Or, even worse, what if there were something — something whose existence she could not even begin to contemplate — waiting for her up ahead? A shudder ran through her, and she turned her head to glance back at the comforting light from her room.

As she stared back at it, she saw the pattern of light grow smaller. Slowly, steadily, the edge of darkness was encroaching upon it.

That's impossible, Kit thought frantically. And then there was the short, strong click of the door coming closed and the entire hall was in darkness.

Steady, Kit told herself firmly. You mustn't panic. The door blew closed, that's all.

But how could it have blown shut when there was no wind? The air in the hall was absolutely still. The stained-glass window at its end was sealed tight.

Should she keep moving forward or turn and work her way back to her room? Just the thought of the bright security of that lighted haven was enough to make her long to reverse her steps. But it would not alter the fact of the scream, of the moaning sob.

There's no way, Kit thought, except to keep going. I've got to find out what's wrong.

Step by cautious step, always keeping one hand upon the wall to orient herself, she moved down the hallway. The floorboards creaked slightly under her feet, and the sound seemed a shriek in the silence. When at last her hand touched the edge of Sandy's door, she drew a deep, shuddering breath of relief.

She groped for the knob and found it. Closing her hand upon it, she tried to turn it. It would not move.

"It's locked!" Kit spoke the words aloud, unable to believe them. How could Sandy possibly have managed to secure the door when the locks were located on the outside? Kit released the knob and rapped hard with her knuckles upon the thick wood. The sound seemed to fill the night.

From somewhere within the room there came a small moan.

"Sandy!" Truly concerned now, Kit called the name aloud. She made her hand into a fist and began to pound upon the door in earnest, heedless of whom else she might wake with the noise. "Sandy, answer me! Are you all right in there? Sandy?"

When there was no answer from within the room she grabbed for the knob again, giving it one final twist out of desperation. To her astonishment, this time it turned quite easily and the door came open. Immediately, a gust of cold air swept upon her, as damp and chilling as though it had come from the Arctic.

"Sandy?" Kit cried, and as she stepped into the room she knew, with a sharp, unexplainable certainty, that her friend was not alone in the dark interior. Someone else was with her.

Fighting a terrible desire to turn and run stumbling and staggering back along the hallway to her own room, Kit groped her way forward. The icy air was all around her, so intense that she found herself growing numb.

"Who is it?" she cried shakily. "Who's in here?"

From somewhere close she could hear the sound of breathing, long heavy breaths as though someone had been running for a long way. The closer she drew to the spot where she knew the bed should be, the more intense the cold became, until she began to wonder if she could bear to move an inch farther. Stretching out her hand, she felt for the edge of the bedside table and then for the lamp that she knew must be standing upon it. It seemed as though her hand was pressing through a wall of ice.

Then she touched the base of the lamp, fumbling along it, and found the button. She pressed it, and immediately the room was filled with blessed light.

Blinking her eyes against the sudden brilliance, Kit glanced wildly about her. The alien presence, if it had ever really existed, was gone. The room fell into place around her, as familiar as her own. The only two people in it were herself and Sandy.

Her friend was sitting straight up in the bed, staring at her. Her eyes had the blank, unfocused look of a sleep-walker, and her skin had a bluish hue, as though she had been outside for a long time in the cold.

Kit reached out tentatively and touched her arm.

"You're frozen!" she said. "My gosh, Sandy, pull up the blanket. What in the world has been going on?"

"Kit?" Sandy spoke the name in a hesitant voice. "Kit, is that you?"

"Of course it's me." Kit tugged the blanket up and hauled it over her friend's shoulders. "Cover up before you get pneumonia. How did your room ever get so cold? Sandy, are you awake? You look so — so odd —"

"Yes. Yes, I guess so." Sandy gave her head a shake as if to rid it of a dream. "What are you doing here? It's the middle of the night."

"It's later than that," Kit said. "I'm here because you yelled. Don't you remember?"

Sandy looked at her blankly. "No. No, I don't. I guess I must have been dreaming."

"Your door was locked."

"It couldn't have been. You know I can't lock it from the inside." Sandy paused, and then repeated Kit's words. "It was locked? My door?"

"It sure was, but then it came free again the second time I tried it. Someone was in here. I could swear it, Sandy. When I stepped into this room I could feel somebody. I don't mean I actually touched him, but you know how it is when you feel a presence, when you know a room isn't empty."

"I was dreaming," Sandy said. Her voice was thin and frightened. "At least, I think I was dreaming. There was this woman by my bed. She was young — maybe in her middle twenties — and she was wearing a long dress, kind of old-fashioned-looking. She was just standing there, looking down at me, and I could see her even in the darkness."

"Good Lord," Kit said. Her legs felt weak, and she sank down on the edge of Sandy's bed. "Of course, you were dreaming. You must have been."

"Yes," Sandy said. "But — but, Kit — it's not the first time."

"It's not?"

"Oh, it's the first time this exact thing has happened. I mean, this woman — a stranger — and the funny clothes and everything. But it's not the first time I've had odd dreams. You know how I told you that I live with my grandparents?"

"Yes."

"My parents died three years ago," Sandy said. "It was their fifteenth wedding anniversary. Daddy had arranged a trip as a surprise for Mother; it was to be a kind of second honeymoon. They were flying to the Bahamas. The plane went down in the ocean. They never even found the wreckage."

"How awful," Kit breathed. "I'm so sorry."

"I was staying with my grandparents," Sandy said. "The crazy thing was — I knew about the plane. I knew

47

it as soon as it happened. I was in the kitchen helping Grandma with the dinner, and suddenly I *knew*. I said, 'Gran, the plane has crashed.' She looked at me as though I were nutty and said, 'What plane?' 'Dad's and Mother's,' I told her. 'It's gone down.' She kept staring at me, and then she said, 'What a terrible thing to joke about!' She was so mad she wouldn't even talk to me, and then, later that night, we heard about it on television."

"You said you had a dream," Kit reminded her.

"It wasn't that night. I don't think any of us slept that night. But the next day after the notification was official, I started crying and couldn't stop, and Grandpa got a doctor over to the house, and he gave me a shot. I did go to sleep then, and that's when I had the dream.

"Daddy and Mother were there, standing next to the bed, holding hands. Mother said, 'Sandy, you've got to get hold of yourself.' In the dream I answered her. I said, 'But, you're dead! I'm crying because you're dead!' And Daddy said, 'Your mother and I are together. To us, that's the important thing. We're happy, and you must be too.' "

Kit looked down at her own hands and saw that they were gripped together until the knuckles were white.

"Did you tell anybody?" she asked.

"I tried to," Sandy said, "but nobody would listen. They just said that everybody has funny dreams when they're emotionally upset."

"They wouldn't believe me either," Kit said quietly.

"You?" Sandy stared at her.

"After my father was killed. Except, I never thought of that as a dream. He was there in my room, *really* there. I know he was."

For a moment they sat in silence, gazing at each other. Sandy's eyes were huge in her thin face and the freckles stood out like polka dots against her pale skin.

Kit was trembling, and this time it was not from cold.

"What does it mean?" Sandy asked finally. "It can't be coincidence. The two of us — both having had experiences like that — and tonight — the locked door — the woman by my bed —"

"I don't know what it means," Kit said. "But I'll tell you one thing. I'm going to do my best to find out."

Chapter 6

They spent the rest of the night in Kit's room.

They did not talk, but Kit was too keyed up to sleep, and she could tell by the sound of her breathing that Sandy was awake also, lying still and tense in the bed beside her. Only when the first flush of dawn lightened the sky beyond the window did she finally doze off, and when she again opened her eyes she found that it was well past eight o'clock and Sandy was no longer in the room.

She got up and dressed and went down to the dining room to breakfast. Ruth and Lynda were there, finishing plates of eggs and toast.

"Yes, Sandy was here a few minutes ago," Ruth told her in answer to her query. "She said she wasn't hungry, she just wanted some coffee, and that she had an early class scheduled with Professor Farley. I guess he's giving her some remedial help in algebra."

"How did she look?" Kit asked.

"Awful," Lynda told her. "I thought maybe she was coming down with something. There were bags under her eyes and she looked exhausted. Come to think of it, you don't look too great yourself." She regarded Kit quizzically. "Is there some sort of flu bug doing the rounds at Blackwood?"

"Not that I know of," Kit said. "We were both up a big part of the night. Sandy had a dream and woke up screaming, and I was in with her for a while, and then she came back to my room with me. Didn't you hear us? Between her yelling and my banging on the door, we should have waked the dead."

Despite herself, she gave a little shiver at her choice of words.

"I didn't hear a thing," Lynda said. "Did you, Ruth?"

"I might have," the dark-haired girl said. "I had a restless night, so maybe I kind of half-consciously got waked up. I've been doing a lot of dreaming myself lately."

"You have?" Kit froze at the statement. "What — what sort of dreams?"

"I don't know," Ruth said with a shrug. "I don't remember them when I wake up. I just have this feeling in the morning that I've been at it all night."

"I know what you mean," Lynda said. "When that alarm goes off, sometimes I can hardly make myself get up."

"Well, at least let's get up from the *table*." Ruth consulted her watch. "We've got literature with Madame in just a couple of minutes. What's on your schedule this morning, Kit?"

"Music," Kit told her.

"And Jules all to yourself? Lucky you!" Lynda giggled and tossed her blond curls. "If I'd known there would be a teacher like him, I'd have signed up for piano lessons too. As it is, I can't even get him to look at me."

"He does seem the silent type," Ruth agreed. "I get the impression he's dedicated to his work. Not that I'm that interested."

"Well, *I* am," Lynda said. "After all, he's probably the only man we're going to see between now and Christmas vacation. That is, unless you count Professor Farley."

The door to the kitchen opened and Natalie came in with a pot of coffee. She nodded a curt good morning, but her face softened a little when she saw Kit.

"Morning, miss," she said. "Can I fix you some breakfast?"

"No thanks, Natalie," Kit said. "I'm not hungry this morning."

Natalie set the coffee pot on the table.

"You ought to eat something," she said. "You're getting skinny."

The aroma of the coffee rose in a cloud, and Kit, who normally found the odor enticing, felt her stomach lurch with a wave of nausea.

"There's no time for it now," she said. "I'm running late. I'll make up for it at lunchtime." With a nod of farewell to the girls, she left the room.

Jules Duret was waiting for her in the music room. He was wearing a pale blue shirt, open at the throat, and a pair of white flared pants. He was seated in a chair by the window, and a musical score lay open on his lap, but he did not seem to be reading it. He had the look of one who had been waiting for a long time.

He glanced up as Kit came in, his face solemn.

"You're late," he said by way of greeting. "I'd about given up on you."

"I'm sorry," Kit said. "I didn't sleep well last night, and I overslept this morning."

It was hard to think of this handsome young man as a teacher. He appeared hardly older than the boys she had gone out with in public school, and his dark good looks made him far more attractive than the best of them. Still, there was a quality of reserve about him that made communication difficult, and Kit, who was usually as at ease with boys as she was with girls, found herself fighting a vague feeling of discomfort in his presence.

"Have you done your practicing?" Jules asked now. "Sit down and let me hear how far you've come. Let's warm up with some scales before we get to the actual pieces."

Kit obediently took her place on the piano bench. She placed her hands on the keys. To her surprise, she found that her fingers were stiff and sore, as though she had already been playing for hours.

"Jules?" she said.

"Yes."

"I — I just don't think I want to play this morning." Kit took her hands from the keys and let them fall into her lap. I'm tired, she thought, I'm so terribly tired, and I'm scared, and I need somebody to talk to. I need a friend.

She raised her eyes to meet the dark, intense gaze of the young man across from her. Was Jules Duret a friend? For all she knew, he might not even like her. Yet whom else was there to talk to? Sandy was as upset as she was, and Lynda and Ruth could provide no help.

"Can we talk for a few minutes," she asked in a thin voice, "instead of having a lesson?"

"Talk?" Jules's eyes seemed to narrow slightly. "About what?"

"Blackwood."

"What about Blackwood?"

"I don't know," Kit said. "That's just it — I don't know. There's something odd about Blackwood, something — sinister. We all of us feel it, but it's almost impossible to put it into words. Things have been happening."

"What do you mean?" Jules asked with interest.

"Well, for one thing, we've all been having dreams. Sandy dreamed last night that someone was in her room. She cried out, and I heard her and went down the hall to find out what was wrong. Her door was locked."

"It couldn't have been," Jules said. "The doors don't lock from the inside."

"Why don't they?" Kit asked.

"What do you mean?"

"Just that. Why don't they lock from the inside the way other doors do? Your mother said that she'd had the locks put on the doors to assure us of privacy, but how can you have privacy if you can't lock up when you're in a room?"

"You can lock up when you go out of a room," Jules said. "So that no one can get into your things while you're gone."

"I'm not concerned about that," Kit said. "I don't have anything sitting around in there valuable enough for someone to want to steal it. But I *would* like to be able to lock the door when I'm inside. And last night, Sandy's door *was* locked. I tried the knob. And then, suddenly, it did come open as though somebody had released it."

"Then it wasn't locked," Jules said with certainty. "It must just have been stuck. I'll see about putting some oil on those latches. Which room did you say it was?"

Kit regarded him with frustration. "Weren't you listening at all? I'm not asking you to oil Sandy's lock — what I'm trying to tell you is that something weird is happening here at Blackwood. There was somebody in Sandy's room last night. A woman. I know it sounds crazy, but Sandy saw her with her own eyes!"

"She was dreaming," Jules said. "You just finished saying yourself that all you girls are doing a lot of that. It's nothing to be concerned about. It often happens to people who are away from home for the first time, under the strain of meeting new people and adjusting to new surroundings." He paused, and then in a lower voice asked, "Did she say anything — the woman in Sandy's room?"

Kit was surprised at the question. "Why do you ask that?"

"Well — just to get the end of the story."

"I don't think she did. At least, Sandy didn't tell me so. What do you care if you're so sure it was a dream?"

"Sandy reacted by screaming," Jules said. "I thought perhaps it was at something the woman had said to her."

"She was frightened," Kit told him, "simply by the fact that the woman was *there*. Can't you imagine what it would be like to wake up in a room where you thought you were all by yourself and find somebody standing by your bed, looking down at you? And the cold — I felt that myself. When I went into the room this great wave of cold air came sweeping over me, and Sandy was blue with it. When I touched her hand, it was like ice."

"Look, Kit," Jules said, "there just couldn't have been a stranger in Sandy's room. How could she have gotten there? The gates to Blackwood are always locked at night, and so is the building itself. Nobody is going to climb up a straight wall to come in a window. And even supposing that were possible, how did she get out again so quickly when you came bursting in the door? Did she have wings?"

"The locked door — the cold air —"

"I told you, the door was undoubtedly stuck. And, of course, the air in Sandy's room was going to be colder than the air in the hallway. She probably had her window open."

Jules leaned over and put his hand on Kit's. It was a

nice hand, warm and strong with long, fine fingers, and it felt good upon hers.

His voice was suddenly gentle. "Blackwood is an old mansion, magnificent, of course, but heavy with atmosphere. Old places are inclined to be that way. You have to get used to this place gradually. I had some dreams myself the first week or so after we came here."

"You did?" Kit asked, surprised.

"Sure. What would you expect? I'm not used to living in a place like Blackwood. I'm fresh out of music school. I've been living in an apartment with a couple of other fellows. I've spent my vacations with my mother at her various schools, but other than that I've pretty much lived my own life. When she wrote and asked if I would come to America with her to teach in her new school, I wasn't too sure I wanted to. Then she told me more about the school — how special it would be and the kind of students she would have here — and I decided to give it a try.

"When I got my first glimpse of Blackwood, I couldn't believe it. I still don't know how my mother was able to locate such a spot. The place has its own vibes. You just have to get used to them."

"And you're used to them now?" Kit asked him.

"I like them. I feel — different — here. I play better. I appreciate things more."

"Do you still dream?"

"Well, sure. Some. Everybody dreams."

"Oh, Jules." Kit tried to smile at him. "You make everything sound so sensible and normal. You must think I'm a fool."

"I don't think that at all," Jules said quietly. "I think you're a smart girl. And a pretty one. Sometimes I wish that I'd met you somewhere else, under another set of circumstances. That I wasn't your teacher. But —" He gave her hand a quick squeeze and released it, "we'll just have to take things as they are. And the way they are right now, we've wasted half the class period chattering. Are you ready to play for me?"

"As ready as I'll ever be," Kit said with a sigh. "I probably have as little talent as anyone you'll ever have as a student. Don't you get bored listening to me plow through pieces like 'Happy Leaves' and 'Swinging on the Gate'?"

"I don't get bored," Jules told her. Then, after a pause, he lowered his voice. "You *do* have talent, Kit. Maybe someday you'll realize how much. There are all sorts of talents in the world, and only one of them is music."

Chapter 7

———————

"Hey, Kit, guess what? I've done your portrait!" Lynda stood in the entrance to the parlor, holding a sheet of paper against her chest.

"You have?" Kit glanced up from her book. "Let's have a look."

The girls generally gathered in the parlor during the hour before dinner. It was a pleasant spot, well lighted with comfortable furnishings, and a good deal more modern than the rest of the rooms at Blackwood.

Usually they chatted or watched television, but tonight no one seemed to be in a communicative mood. Kit and Ruth had been reading, and Sandy was over at the card table in the corner, dealing out a game of solitaire.

Now, with Lynda's entrance, they all looked up from their activities. There was something about Lynda's bright prettiness that wakened any room, and at this moment she looked so innocently pleased with herself that Kit found herself smiling.

"Come on, let's see it. I didn't know you were an artist."

"I didn't either," Lynda said, handing her the paper. "I really surprised myself."

Kit held the sketch out in front of her in a joking manner and then caught her breath in amazement. "Why — it *is* of me!"

"I told you it was." Lynda perched on the arm of her chair. "Do you like it?"

"Like it!" Kit exclaimed. "Why, it's — it's — incredible. I mean it, honestly. Lynda, you're great!"

"This I've got to see." Ruth got up from the couch and came over to stand behind them. She was silent a moment and then said, "You couldn't have drawn that, Lynda. You must have traced it or something."

"I didn't," Lynda said in a hurt voice. "I just sat down and drew it. I'd been taking a nap, and I woke up, and all of a sudden I wanted to draw a picture. I went over to the desk and got a pencil and a sheet of paper and sat down and did it, just like that. And the funny thing is, I didn't even know who it was going to be until it started to look like Kit, and then suddenly it *was* Kit."

"But you've never done any drawing before," Ruth said skeptically. "You never took art classes in school. This sketch — well, it's expert. The eyes have that direct, kind of challenging look that Kit's do, and the mouth — the chin — everything — it's Kit, all over. It's absolutely professional."

By this time Sandy too had come over and was studying the picture.

"You're right," she said. "It's awfully good. Would you do one of me, Lynda? I'd like to send it to my grandparents. I bet they'd frame it."

"Sure," Lynda said happily. "Now that I've caught the knack of how to do this, I'll draw everybody. Next I think I'll do Madame Duret with her eyes kind of boring right into you, the way they do. Or maybe Jules. Would anybody like a picture of him?"

"Do carbons of that one," Kit said with a laugh.

59

"We're all going to want them. And one of Professor Farley stroking his beard —"

"Did I hear my name mentioned?" The professor's deep voice broke into the conversation. He stood framed in the doorway, smiling in his friendly way. "Let me in on the joke. I was drawn by the laughter."

"I was drawn too," Kit said, "but in my case, it was by a pencil." She turned the picture so that he could see it. "Look what Lynda did. Isn't that something?"

"It is, indeed." Professor Farley came slowly into the room to stand, gazing down at the penciled portrait. "That's an excellent piece of work, Lynda. Have you studied art for a long time?"

"I've never studied it at all," Lynda told him. "In fact, the only drawing I've ever done was during a party game once when we were all supposed to draw each other and then have people guess who the pictures were. I drew Ruth, and won the booby prize."

"Well, you've surely improved since then," Professor Farley said admiringly. "I'm going to mention this to Madame Duret. She likes to encourage talent in our young people. I'm sure she will provide you with art supplies that will allow you to express yourself better than you can with a pencil."

"May I keep this?" Kit asked, and Lynda nodded, pleased.

"Of course. I'm glad you like it enough to want it. And I will do you, Sandy, and you too, Ruth, if you want me to. Or do you still believe that I traced?"

"No," Ruth said apologetically. "I've never known you to lie about anything. Besides, what could you possibly have traced it from? I'm sorry to have sounded so doubtful. It's just that we've known each other so long, and to suddenly discover that you're an artist comes as a shock. It's as though I've never really known you at all."

"You know me better than anybody," Lynda said fondly. "I'd never have made it through at that last boarding school if it hadn't been for your helping me. Like I said, I don't wonder you're surprised. I'm surprised myself."

"Five minutes till dinner," Kit said, glancing at her watch. "I'm going to run upstairs and put this picture in my room before something happens to it. The way we're thumbing it over, it's going to be nothing but one big smudge."

The soft glow of twilight lit the stained-glass window at the end of the hall with a gentle radiance that made the hallway itself appear like the center aisle of a cathedral.

At a moment like this, Kit thought as she walked down it, I can almost believe that all the creepiness has been in my imagination.

She reached the door of her room and opened it and went in. She flicked on the study light and laid the pencil portrait on the desk.

For a long moment she stood there, gazing down at it. It was not an intricate sketch; the lines were pure and simple, and yet it caught something beyond a surface likeness. The straight nose, the stubborn chin, the curve of the rounded cheek, all were there, but there was something more, something about the eyes. As Ruth had commented, they had a directness which was typical of Kit, but there was another quality too — a youngness, a touch of uncertainty. The eyes were those of a girl who was not as sure on the inside as she appeared outwardly to be.

"Who am I?" the eyes asked. "What is my place in life? Am I pretty? Do people like me? Does *Jules* like me? In what direction am I going? Will I accomplish anything worthwhile in my lifetime? Will I be happy? Am I worth loving?"

A multitude of questions glimmered behind the eyes, suggested by a few tiny lines and some subtle shading. It was the difference between the real Kit, the one known only to herself and possibly to Tracy, and the strong, self-confident Kathryn Gordy everyone else saw.

How did she guess? Kit asked herself wonderingly. How in the world could Lynda Hannah come to know me so well? We've never talked with each other except as part of a group.

But the girl in the picture could not be denied.

"Kit?" Sandy's voice called to her from the stairs at the end of the hall. "Madame's rung the bell for dinner. Come along or you're going to be late."

"Coming," Kit called back.

Flicking off the light, she left the room, pulling the door closed behind her. She hesitated a second and then, turning back, she reentered the room and took the key off the bureau top, where it had lain ever since Madame had given it to her upon her arrival at Blackwood, and went out again into the hall.

This time she thrust the key into the lock and turned it. She did not know exactly why, but for the first time since she had come here, she felt that her room held something of value.

Dinner hour was one of the pleasantest times at Blackwood. All meals were served in the grandeur of the dining room, but only the evening meal was eaten by candlelight with a white cloth upon the table and linen napkins and fine china. The dishes were pure white and thin to the touch, and each plate was bordered by a delicate line of gold.

"They came with Blackwood," Madame Duret explained when Kit asked about them. "The dishes and

62

kitchenware, the furniture, the piano, the drapes and carpets, all of them have been here for years and years. The only things that were brought in from outside were the furnishings in my own apartment, which I had shipped over after I closed my school in England, and those in the reconverted carriage house which was made into an apartment for Professor Farley. And, of course, the furnishings in the rooms occupied by you girls."

"It's strange," Kit commented, examining the china, "that something so lovely would just have been left here. You'd think the owners would have wanted it for themselves."

"It is strange," Madame had agreed, "but then, people are peculiar sometimes, are they not? After Mr. Brewer died the new owners wanted nothing to do with Blackwood except to sell it. It is a shame, really, but very lucky for us."

The china set the mood of dinner. It was an elegant meal, served in several courses, and Madame Duret seemed at that time less a headmistress than a gracious hostess, entertaining her guests with interesting stories of her life abroad. Jules occasionally contributed to these, as did Professor Farley, who had taught at Madame's school in England though not at the one in France. Conversation flowed freely, with all of the girls joining in, and dinner generally ended with everyone in good spirits, ready to adjourn to the parlor or to go up to her room to study.

This night was different. The atmosphere in the dining room seemed charged with an extra quality, a kind of electricity. Conversation moved well, as always, but to Kit there seemed to be an artificiality about it, as though the speakers were playing their parts and did not really have their minds on the discussion. At one point she caught an exchange of glances between Madame and Professor Farley. As far as she could see, there had been nothing to trigger it, but when Madame Duret turned back again her eyes were shining with a kind of suppressed excitement. Or perhaps it was simply the flicker of the candles reflected in the black pupils.

When dinner was over and Kit had started down the hall to the stairs, Sandy caught up with her and laid a hand on her arm.

"Let's go out for a little while," she said softly.

"Out? At night? Whatever for?" Kit asked her.

"Just into the garden. I need to talk. Please?"

"All right," Kit said. "But we'd better slip out through the kitchen. I'm sure Madame wouldn't want us roaming around the grounds in the dark."

Natalie was putting away the silver when they entered. She glanced up sharply.

"Where do you ladies think you're going?"

"Out," Kit told her. "For air." Natalie's crispness had never bothered Kit, for she knew that the girl liked her and that this was simply her manner.

"I don't blame you," Natalie said now. "It's stuffy in this place. The rest of the help is quitting."

"You're kidding!" Kit exclaimed. "Why?"

"They just don't like it, especially the upstairs part. They say it spooks 'em, cleaning in that hall. One girl says she gets headaches."

"Are you quitting?" Kit asked.

"Not me. I need the job. I got myself and a sick dad to support. Besides, I don't go along with all that superstition stuff. Whatever happened was so long ago, you can't count it."

"What do you mean?" Kit's curiosity was piqued. "What happened here?"

"Oh, well, Mr. Brewer was sort of odd." Natalie gave

64

a shrug. "People blow things up. Will you be warm enough outside? My coat and sweater are in the broom closet if you want to wear them."

"Thanks," Kit said gratefully. "We won't be outside long."

Giving the coat to Sandy, she herself pulled on the worn blue sweater that hung on a nail on the inside of the closet door, and the two girls let themselves out into the night.

The path from the kitchen door led around the corner of the house and into the garden. There was a three-quarter moon hanging high over the trees, sending long bands of silver out across the lawn. The garden path was aglow with moonlight, and a faint, sweet smell rose from the bushes, as though in remembrance of recent summer flowers. Below the lawn the pond lay black and still with the moonlight making a silver path across its surface.

The night air was cold and pure, tinged with the scent of trees. The woods rose in a dark frame around the silver garden and shining pond.

"How lovely," Kit said softly. "I'm glad you wanted to come outside. It's even more beautiful at night than it is in the daytime."

"I had to come," Sandy said. "If I'd stayed cooped up inside those walls any longer I think I'd have strangled. Kit, am I crazy? What on earth is happening to me?"

"You mean, your dream?" Kit tried to sound reassuring. "I talked with Jules about that, and what he said made a lot of sense. You're away from home for the first time, adjusting to new things —"

"That's not it," Sandy interrupted. "It really isn't, I'm sure of it. It's this place — Blackwood itself. There's something weird about Blackwood. Don't tell me you haven't felt it too. I know you have."

"Well, sure —" Kit found her thoughts swept back to

65

that first day as she and her mother and Dan saw the mansion standing before them, huge and stark with the late afternoon sunlight glancing off the windows to make the whole place seem aflame from within.

"Can't you feel it?" she had cried to Dan and her mother. "There's something about the place — something —"

"Yes," she said to Sandy now, shivering a little despite the wool sweater. "I did say that, and I do know what it is that you're saying. But how can it be the place itself? A place doesn't have a personality."

"What was the first word that came to your mind when you saw it?"

"I — I don't remember —" Kit began.

"You do. You just don't want to remember. There was a particular word, and it jumped right into your mind. It was 'evil.'"

"You're right." Kit turned to her incredulously. "How could you know that? I never told you. I never told anybody."

"I know it because the word was *there*. I felt it too. It was as much a part of the first view of this place as the peaked roof. Professor Farley picked me up at the bus stop in the village, and we drove up here through the beautiful morning with the sunlight streaming down through the trees and the sky so blue and clear. We came through the gate and started up the driveway, and it was as though a black shadow fell in front of us. An invisible shadow. The closer we got to the house, the darker it became — the kind of darkness you can feel and not see — and when I got out of the car and walked through that front door, I almost turned and ran back out again."

"But — but we don't feel it now," Kit said. "Not all the time. At night along the hall we do, with it all so black — and in our dreams — but there are lots of times when we laugh and study and go to class and it's all so nice and normal —"

"Because we're part of it now," Sandy said. "Don't you see, Kit? We're *part* of the shadow. We've been living in it for weeks and we're adjusting to it. That's why I wanted to come outside tonight, to stand back from Blackwood and be able to look at it and feel the difference."

"It does feel different from out here," Kit admitted. Standing there in the moonlight, she could look at Blackwood, at the great building with the pointed roof, towering against the paler darkness of the sky, as though it were a picture in a child's storybook. Sandy's second-floor corner room was dark. A light shone in Ruth's; evidently she had already begun her evening studying. Lynda's room was on the far side of the hall, facing off the other side of the house. And her own —

"There's a light on," she said.

"What?"

"A light in my room. There — that window there — that *is* my room, isn't it?"

"Of course," Sandy said. "Perhaps you left it on when you came down to dinner."

"I didn't," Kit said. "I remember turning the light off. Then I locked the door." She stiffened, her eyes glued to the shining window, as a dark form moved across it.

"Somebody's there!" she exclaimed. "Somebody's in my room!"

"That's impossible if you locked your door." Sandy too was staring at the window. "Maybe it's the curtain blowing."

"It's not! It's a person!" Kit whirled and started up the path at a run. "Come on, we'll catch him! There's no

67

place he can go except back along the hall. If we get to the stairs in time we can cut him off!"

But the stairs were empty, and so was the long, black hallway. The door was still locked. When she turned the key and opened it, Kit found the room dark.

She turned on the light, and before she looked, she knew what she would find. The pencil portrait was no longer on her desk.

Her dream that night was different. It was a strange dream, and oddly lovely. In it she was in the music room, sitting at the piano, and her fingers were at home on the keys. There was no sheet music in front of her, but she was playing in a way that she had never played before. It was a beautiful melody, as cool and haunting as the moonlight in the garden, as smooth as the path of silver across the pond.

It is so beautiful, she told herself in the dream, that I must try to remember it so that I can play it again. But the music had no name, and she knew that she had never before heard it.

When she woke in the morning she felt as exhausted as though she had never slept at all, and her fingers ached.

Chapter 8

The incoming mail was on a table in the entrance hall, and Kit, coming back from a class with Professor Farley, picked up her portion and carried it up to her room to read.

There were two postcards from her mother, one from Cherbourg and one from Paris, both sent airmail but with a week between mailing dates.

". . . so exciting," the first one said, ". . . marvelous trip over . . . so many interesting people on board . . . we caught up on our sleep and lay out on deck chairs." The second was filled with references to the Eiffel Tower and Montmartre and the Folies Bergères.

"Where are your letters, honey?" said a hurried postscript. "We got your note in Cherbourg but haven't had a word since. You have our itinerary. Write care of American Express, but allow enough time."

Besides the postcards, there was a letter from Tracy. The neat, round handwriting, almost as familiar as Tracy herself, gave Kit a momentary pang of homesickness.

"That must be some great place," the letter ran, "if you can't even get around to writing. What's with that promise you made to keep me up to date on everything? Things here are as usual. I got Mrs. Logan for English — hooray! — and Mr. Garfield for Latin — ugh. Advanced art is keen, we can do whatever we want. There's a cute guy in my geometry class named Kevin Weber. How are you bearing up at Blackwood without a single guy under the age of eighty?"

There's Jules, Kit thought. I wrote her about Jules in my very first letter. Could it be that it got lost in the mail? But I've written a couple of times since and mentioned him both times.

She flipped over the page and was skimming the next few paragraphs when there was a light rap at the door.

"Come on in," Kit called, assuming it was Sandy. To her surprise her visitor turned out to be Ruth Stark.

"I hope I'm not disturbing you." The dark-haired girl stood hesitantly in the doorway. "If you're in the middle of studying —"

"I'm not," Kit said. "I'm only reading some letters."

"Then I want to show you something." Ruth stepped inside and closed the door carefully behind her. "It's this."

She held out a sheet of paper. At a glance Kit could see that it was a crude sketch of a face, a wavering, childish drawing of the type that one might expect to see in a display of grammar school art.

"What is it?" she asked. "Did it come in the mail? Your little brother or sister —"

"No," Ruth said. "It's a portrait of me. Lynda did it. It's the picture she drew for that parlor game she was talking about."

"Lynda drew that?" Kit exclaimed, reaching for the paper and laying it flat on the bed in front of her. Ruth came over to stand beside her and together they studied the drawing. A round, unformed face. A triangle nose. A mouth that resembled a Halloween pumpkin. A mop of black hair.

"She got the hair right," Ruth said. "It's black. Frankly, I don't see any other resemblance. I know I'm no beauty queen, but even *I* have two eyes that look in the same direction. And she's forgotten to put on the ears."

"I don't understand," Kit said. "We know that Lynda can draw. That portrait she did of me was excellent."

"It was a freak," Ruth said flatly. "Lynda can't draw. Lynda doesn't have any talent in anything. She's pretty and sweet, but the day they distributed brains, Lynda was out to lunch."

Somehow from Ruth the statement did not sound brutal, simply factual.

"Sit down," Kit said slowly. "I think you and I need to talk."

Ruth nodded. She seated herself on the edge of the bed. In her lap, her square, strong hands gripped each other tightly.

"Something's going on here," she said in a low voice. "I'm aware of it, but I don't know what it is. Do you feel it too?"

"Yes," Kit said, "and so does Sandy."

"Lynda doesn't. Lynda just doesn't notice things. She's like a little kid in so many ways."

"Maybe you'd better tell me about her," Kit said. "And about yourself. The two of you seem to be good friends, but you're so different. There's nothing wrong with *your* I.Q."

"It's a hundred and fifty," Ruth said with pride. "I was ahead of myself from the beginning. I skipped two grades in grammar school, and by the time I reached junior high I'd already read so far ahead on my own that the things in the textbooks were old stuff to me. And the kids didn't like me. Who wants a fat little nine-year-old in a class of twelve-year-olds?

"My parents are both Ph.D.s. They think education is awfully important, so they decided to send me to a special, ungraded school in Los Angeles. That's where I first met Lynda Hannah."

"What was she doing there," Kit asked, "if the school was for brilliant students?"

"Well, it wasn't exactly. At least, that's what I discovered after I got there. It was just 'elite.' I don't know if you realize it or not, but Lynda's mother is Margaret Storm."

"Margaret Storm, the actress?" Kit said in surprise. "I've seen her on some of the late movies on television."

"She was pretty popular in her day," Ruth said. "Of course, a glamorous actress doesn't stay on top forever. Lynda says she's still making pictures, but the parts aren't that good anymore, and she met some Italian actor in one of them and there was some sort of scandal — well, anyway, she's living in Italy now. That's why Lynda was away at school. She was really lost there; she'd try and try and she just couldn't keep up academically. And I couldn't keep up socially. We sort of found each other, and after that it wasn't so bad for either of us."

"Why did you come to Blackwood?" Kit asked her.

"That was my parents' doing. They didn't think the school in L.A. was challenging enough, and they were right. When they read the brochure about Blackwood and saw the part about the private instruction, the way each student moves along at her own level, they got pretty excited. We talked about it during spring vacation, and Mother wrote Madame Duret and arranged for me to take the entrance tests, and then Lynda heard about it and persuaded her mother to let her take them too. She didn't want to be left behind."

"And she got in?" Kit said. "That's surprising, isn't it."

"I couldn't believe it," Ruth said. "I thought maybe they'd mixed up the scores. But Lynda likes it here. Everybody's nice to her. And now suddenly she thinks she's an artist, and she's thrilled about that. Madame Duret has given her an easel and oil paints and canvases. You should see Lynda's room! It looks like a professional studio."

"But if she doesn't have art ability," Kit said, "how could she have drawn the picture of me? You call it a 'freak,' but that's no answer. How could someone produce something as expert as that, when the best she has ever done before is *this*?" She gestured toward the dreadful sketch.

"That's what's so crazy," Ruth said. "Maybe that picture of you isn't as good as we first thought it was. Why don't you go get it so we can look at it again?"

"I can't," Kit said. "I don't have it any longer."

"You don't have it?"

"Somebody took it," Kit said. "The door was locked, but somebody got in anyway and took the picture off my desk."

"Do you know who?" Ruth asked her.

"No. I can't imagine. I can't even think who would want the picture. We all have the keys to our own rooms, but I'm sure that Madame must have duplicates. Who could get hold of one of them depends upon where she keeps them."

"Or she could have used one herself," Ruth suggested.

"Why in the world would she do a thing like that? Why would a picture of me mean that much to her? Besides, as far as I know, she wasn't even aware of the

73

sketch. She wasn't in the parlor when Lynda brought it in to show to us. Nobody was there then except us girls."

"Professor Farley came in," Ruth reminded her. "He saw it."

"That's right, he did. But why would *he* want it? The more we talk about it, the more ridiculous the whole thing seems. Lynda, who can't draw, draws a wonderful picture. There's no reason for anyone to want it except me, yet somebody goes into a locked room to steal it. Add to that Sandy's nightmare about the woman by her bed —"

"A nightmare?"

"That's what Jules thinks it was. Sandy isn't so certain. She's had experiences like that before. There was one in particular, right after her parents were killed. They were in a plane crash, and before any report was received, Sandy knew about it. She says it just came to her from out of the blue, the absolute certainty that the plane was down and her parents were dead."

"So she has it too." Ruth spoke softly, and there was no surprise in her voice.

"Has what?" Kit asked blankly.

"ESP." Ruth paused, and then, seeing the bewilderment on Kit's face, elaborated. "Extrasensory perception. It's a sort of sixth sense that some people are born with. It's a special kind of sensitivity to things that are normally not seen or heard."

"And you think Sandy has that?" Kit exclaimed. "But you said, 'she has it *too*.' Do you mean that *you* —"

"I've had it for as long as I remember," Ruth said. "For a while I didn't realize what it was. I thought maybe it just came with being bright, my being able to sense things that other people couldn't. It was part of how I got ahead so fast in school. I could look at a book and sometimes I wouldn't even have to open it, I'd find I

74

knew without reading it what was inside. When my teachers asked questions, I'd know the answers even if I hadn't studied the material. I could feel the answers in their minds. Then I'd tell them just what it was they wanted to hear."

"And Lynda?" Kit asked shakily. "Does Lynda have this ability too?"

"Not in the same way," Ruth said. "With Lynda it's a different thing. Lynda remembers."

"Remembers?" Kit repeated the word stupidly. "Remembers *what*?"

"This is going to sound crazy," Ruth said. "It did to me the first time she told me. But, now — after coming to know her so well — I swear, I almost believe it's true. At least, I believe that Lynda thinks it is."

"Well?"

Ruth's eyes dropped to her hands, still gripped tightly in her lap.

"Lynda," she said, "remembers another lifetime in which she was born in England and lived under Queen Victoria."

"Good grief!" Kit said in a cracked voice. There was a long moment of silence while she digested this information. Then she shook her head. "You're right, it's crazy. But it's no crazier than the night I woke to see my father standing by my bed. In the morning I found that he had been killed in an accident the night before."

"So —" Ruth said softly, "it's you too." She drew a deep breath. "I guess that now, at least, we realize what it is the four of us girls have in common, and why, out of all the applications, we were selected to be the first students at Blackwood."

At first the thought occurred to her that she might be dreaming again. Of course, she knew that she wasn't. It

was midafternoon, and she was on her way to her literature class with Madame Duret. And yet, the music —

It was coming from behind the closed door of the
music room. Strange and beautiful and achingly familiar,
the melody swept over her, drawing from her a response
she had never experienced from any music before.

She placed her hand on the knob and opened the door.
Jules was seated with his back toward her, operating the
tape recorder.

"What are you playing?" Kit asked him. When he did
not respond, she realized that he was concentrating too
hard upon the music to have heard her. She raised her
voice. "Jules, what is that music?"

With a quick, startled gesture, Jules flicked the play-
back switch and the tape slowed to a halt. His expression
when he turned was one of unreasonable anger.

"What do you mean, interrupting —" he began, and
then, at the sight of Kit's surprised face, he seemed to
catch himself. His voice softened. "Oh — it's you."

"You didn't have to shut it off," Kit said. "I heard the
music through the door. It's beautiful. I had to know —
what is it called?"

"I don't think it has a name," Jules told her.

"But it must. Everything that's published has a name."

"Well, sure. What I meant was, I don't know what it
is."

"Doesn't it say on the tape?"

"It's not a commercial tape," Jules said. "It's just a
collection of odds and ends I've taken from one place or
another because I liked them."

"I like them too," Kit said. "Especially that last piece.
Could you play it again?"

"You heard most of it." Jules made no gesture to reach
again for the switch of the recorder.

Kit regarded him with bewilderment. Never had she seen Jules Duret any way but in complete control of himself. Now he looked off balance, as though he did not know how to handle the situation.

His eyes shifted from hers in a way that made him look almost guilty.

Guilty — about what? Kit could not imagine. She knew that she should continue to class. She was already late, and Madame could not stand tardiness.

Still, she stood there, anchored in the doorway, watching the play of expressions on Jules's handsome face.

"You do know that song," she said with certainty. "You're a music graduate. If you don't recall the title, you must at least know who wrote it. Who was the composer?"

"I'm not sure," Jules said. "It sounds like — well, I guess it's from something by Schubert."

"By Schubert? And you don't recognize it?" Kit was incredulous. "How can you possibly not know the work of someone so famous?"

"*You* don't recognize it," Jules said defensively.

"No, but I don't claim to be a student of music. Even so, I know that Schubert died when he was very young. He couldn't have written that much."

"Look, Kit —" Jules did meet her gaze now. His eyes were blazing, and the anger which he had shown when he had first turned and seen her lay somewhere in their depths. "I don't know what's gotten into you all of a sudden, but I don't need this kind of interrogation. You don't know a thing about music. You can't have heard this music before. It's practically unknown."

"But I have heard it," Kit said quietly.

She had not only heard it, but she knew where it had been. The melody on the tape was the same haunting song that she had been playing in her dream.

Chapter 9

———◆———

In October, Lynda completed a landscape and Sandy wrote a poem.

The landscape was done in oils. It was a large canvas, measuring two feet tall by three and a half feet wide. It was of a lake, serene and peaceful, throwing back the golden glint of the afternoon sun. The woods on the far side of the water were in shadow, but the immediate foreground was bright with sunlight and wild flowers.

"Where is it?" Kit asked.

"It's in the Catskills," Lynda said.

"A place you've been?"

"I don't think so. I know how it looks though." Lynda regarded the painting with pride. "Don't you think it's pretty?"

Kit nodded. The picture was very good indeed.

"Lynda —" Ruth spoke gently, as one might to a small child. "I want you to think a minute. Try to remember what it was that made you decide to paint this particular scene. Did it come from a calendar, maybe? Or did you once see it on television?"

"I don't know," Lynda said. She frowned, considering

the question. "It's a funny thing, but I don't remember thinking about it at all. I just mixed the paints and took the brush in my hand, and I started painting."

"How did you know how to mix the colors?"

"That's not hard."

"Could you teach me?"

"No," Lynda said. "You just have to know it by yourself. I can do it, but I couldn't explain how to somebody else." She smiled apologetically, that sweet, bland smile that made her look so much younger than her actual years. "I'm sorry, Ruth. I guess a person just happens to be a natural artist, or she doesn't."

She showed the oil to Madame Duret, who admired it greatly and hung it on the wall in the dining room. In the week that followed, Lynda produced two more paintings, small ones. Both were landscapes. One seemed to be of the same lake, but from a different angle, for it showed a footpath leading down to its edge. The other was of fields, green with springtime, lying flat and rich beneath a blue sky.

In the bottom right-hand corner of each picture, Lynda printed the initials T.C.

"T.C.?" Kit said. "Those aren't your initials."

"That's the way I'm going to sign my work," Lynda told her.

"But, why? What do they stand for?" Kit was bewildered.

"Nothing really. I just picked the initials out of the air. People don't have to paint under their regular names, and I'm going to paint under T.C."

It was soon after this that Sandy wrote the poem.

"I did this," she said without preliminaries, tossing herself across the foot of Kit's bed and handing her a sheet of lined paper which had evidently been torn from a spiral notebook. "Read it and tell me what you think."

It was late afternoon and Kit, who was tired of studying, tossed her book aside and picked up the poem. It was titled "Leavetaking."

Quickly she scanned it and then went back to read it again:

I never thought it would be Paradise.
I walked a rugged pathway from the start.
No Ugliness was hidden from my eyes,
Nor was Life's pain a stranger to my heart.
And yet, the earth sprung firm beneath my feet
And summer winds were gentle to my hair.
I breathed upon the dusk, and found it sweet,
I gazed upon the dawn and found it fair.
I know gray moors where shadow mists lie curled
And sunbright streams and night skies rich with stars.
For all its faults, I so have loved this World
And found it beautiful, despite its scars.
Though Angels sing of Glories greater still,
I leave in Sadness, much against my will.

"You wrote that?" Kit turned to her friend in amazement. "Why, Sandy, it's just — just —"

"You don't have to say it," Sandy interrupted. "I know it's good. I also know I didn't make it up."

"You remembered it from somewhere?"

"I must have," Sandy said. "I couldn't have written it myself. On the other hand, I don't recall ever having read it. I never read poetry unless it's for a class assignment."

"I certainly don't recognize it," Kit said. "Perhaps Ruth will know what it's from. She's awfully well read." She started to get to her feet, but Sandy reached out a restraining hand.

"Let's not bring Ruth into this."

Kit was surprised. "Why not?"

"I just don't care for her," Sandy said. "There's something about her that turns me off. I can't put my finger on what it is, but I have this feeling that down inside she's a cold fish and that the only person in life who really matters to her is Ruth Stark."

"She's terribly smart," Kit said.

"I'll give you that. She makes me feel like a moron. Still —" Sandy drew a long breath. "I'm being silly, I guess. Okay, go get her. If this is from something famous, she'll probably know what it is."

Ruth, however, did not recognize the poem.

"It's a type of sonnet," she said, studying the paper. "It has a familiar ring to it, but I've never read it." She glanced across at Sandy. "Where did you get it?"

When Sandy did not answer, Kit spoke for her.

"She wrote it this afternoon."

"Then why —" Ruth stopped as the meaning of the statement became clear to her. Her sharp, dark eyes took on a sparkle of interest. "How did it happen, Sandy? Do you write poetry often?"

"Never," Sandy said shortly. "And I don't know one kind of sonnet from another. That's what's so crazy. I went up to my room after lunch and stretched out on my bed to check over some algebra problems. I must have dozed off, because suddenly I realized that a lot of time had gone by. I had a pencil in my hand, and on the page of my notebook opposite the math problems there was this poem."

" 'Leavetaking,' " Ruth read the title again. Her face was flushed with suppressed excitement. "First Lynda — and now you. It's really incredible."

"What does Lynda have to do with this?" Kit asked her.

"Don't you see a connection? Lynda's never painted

81

before, and yet she suddenly seems to have this marvelous talent and is turning out pictures that look as though they belong in museums. Sandy's never written poetry, and here she is writing sonnets. And I —"

She paused. Kit regarded her in bewilderment.

"And you?"

"I've been doing some pretty intricate math," Ruth said carefully, "stuff I could never even have conceived of before. At first I thought I was just writing down a lot of numbers. I couldn't see any meaning in them. But now I'm beginning to get glimmers of understanding. It's as though I were being educated by a teacher who is more — much more — capable than Professor Farley."

"What exactly are you driving at?" Sandy's face was dead white beneath her freckles. "Are you trying to say that this is something supernatural?"

Ruth gave her a challenging look. "Do you have a better explanation?"

"Any explanation is better than that," Sandy said shakily.

"There was that woman," Ruth said, "that night in your room when Kit heard you screaming. And there was the time after your parents' death when you knew about the plane crash. If those weren't supernatural occurrences, I'd like to know what you would call them."

"You told her about those things?" Sandy turned to Kit accusingly. "I told you about them in confidence."

"I'm sorry," Kit said. "I didn't think of them as secrets. All these things are part of the mystery of Blackwood. We have to compare our experiences. Perhaps then we'll see some kind of pattern. Ruth thinks that all four of us girls are very sensitive to ESP sort of things, and that that's how we came to be chosen as students here."

"Those entrance exams we took," Sandy said thoughtfully. "They *were* kind of unusual." She paused. "Then, if that should be true — if we were selected for that particular reason — it means that Madame Duret —"

She could not bring herself to complete the sentence. Ruth finished it for her. "It means that Madame Duret wanted us at Blackwood for exactly that reason."

The room was silent as they digested this statement. Kit thought, this can't be real, this conversation. We're making this up, the three of us; we're inventing a story and giving ourselves roles in it, the way Tracy and I used to do when we were younger.

But she was no longer twelve, and Tracy was not here, and Ruth was not one to play games. Sandy was not playing either; her thin face looked sick.

"We'll have to ask her," Sandy said in a half whisper.

"Ask Madame Duret?" Ruth shook her head. "There'd be nothing to gain by that. Any question we put to her, she's bound to have an answer for. We don't have proof that there's anything wrong. So Lynda's painting and Sandy's turned into a poet — what does that prove? Only that Blackwood is a good school and is bringing out latent talents in its students."

"It's the same with your math," Kit said. "She'll just credit Professor Farley for being such a good instructor. I seem to be the only one here who hasn't developed a new talent." She tried to make her voice light. "I feel sort of left out."

"I wish *I* were left out," Sandy said. "This whole thing's creepy. If we can't ask Madame Duret outright, then what *can* we do? If Ruth's theory is right and we're all reacting because we're sensitive personalities, then I want to know what it is we're reacting to. I'm the same person I was when I was back home, but I didn't write poetry then. Why am I doing it here at Blackwood? Is it something about the place itself?"

"What do we know about Blackwood?" Ruth asked.

"Other than the fact that it's an old estate? I don't even know the name of the family that used to own it."

"I know that," Kit volunteered. "It's Brewer. But that doesn't help much."

"I can see no way of getting into town to ask about it," Sandy said. "We haven't been out of this enclosure since we got here. It's a good fifteen miles down to the village, which is farther than I'm about to hike."

"You couldn't get out anyway," Kit said. "The gate's kept closed except when Professor Farley drives down to the town for mail. What about the village help that works here?"

"What help?" Ruth said. "They all quit except for Natalie Culler, and she never opens her mouth."

"She does with me sometimes," Kit said. "We got to be friends on that first day before the rest of you arrived."

"Well, there's nothing to lose," Ruth conceded, "if you want to raise the question to her. The worst she can do is refuse to answer."

"I'll do it," Kit said determinedly, "as soon as I get the chance."

That night it rained. It was a heavy, relentless rain that drummed upon the roof and slashed against the panes and poured in torrents through the rain gullys.

Lying in bed, Kit closed her eyes tightly and tried to pretend that it was a city rain, and that she was in her room at home and the roof above her head was a simple partition that separated her from the next floor of apartments, and that her mother was in the room next door reading, wearing her blue lace bedjacket, with cold cream smeared across her cheeks. In a moment, Kit thought, she will lay her book aside and get out of bed and come into my room to check the window.

But when the bedroom door did open, it was not her mother who slipped through and pushed it closed behind her. "Kit," a voice asked softly, "are you awake?"

"Yes," Kit said. "What is it? Is something wrong? Wait a minute, I'll turn on the light."

"No, don't," Sandy said. "I just want to tell you something. The woman — her name is Ellis."

"The woman in your dream? You've given her a name?"

"Kit, it wasn't a dream." Sandy sounded definite. "It's something else — something more than a dream. This isn't something my mind's made up. Ellis exists. She's a real person. I'm sure of it."

"That's impossible," Kit said. She reached out in the dark and began to fumble for the bedside lamp.

"Don't," Sandy said, sensing her action. "Please, don't. As long as it stays dark I can still see her like a picture on the screen of my mind. She's young — even younger than I thought at first — and she has the most beautiful eyes, dreamy and filled with sorrow as though she's been through a lot of suffering."

"You were afraid of her that first time," Kit said. "You screamed."

"Not now. I'm not afraid any longer. I just wanted to tell you that." Her footsteps brushed on the floor. "Good night, Kit."

The bedroom door opened and closed. Alone once more, Kit shivered and pulled the blankets up over her shoulders. The room was heavy with dampness and the slow, hard beat of the rain.

Chapter 10

The opportunity to talk with Natalie did not come immediately. It was not until several days later, in the evening after dinner, that Kit saw her chance.

The meal had been a subdued one without the usual conversation. Jules had eaten early and driven into town for the evening. Professor Farley had not come to dinner, as he was engaged in doing some writing and did not wish to be disturbed.

"This is how it is with professors," Madame Duret explained lightly. "They must always be publishing something. Perhaps the day will come when some of you girls will be doing the same thing."

Lynda was not at the table either. She had sent word by Ruth that she was not feeling well, and Madame said that a tray should be carried up to her.

"I'll take it," Kit offered, as they were being excused from the table.

"That is kind of you, Kathryn," Madame said. She paused, as though about to add something, and then evidently decided against it.

As she climbed the stairs, Kit realized that it had been

weeks since she had last been inside Lynda's room. The last time she had seen it, she had been impressed by its femininity. The bureau top had been a field of cosmetics, artificial roses had blossomed in a vase on the desk, and the mirror had been edged with a full circle of photographs, all of Lynda herself, smiling coyly up at a variety of admiring boys. The romantic novels that Lynda loved to read had stood in a row on the bedside table, flanked by delicately carved gilt bookends, and a pajama bag, shaped like a pink kitten, had been propped on the pillow of the bed.

Now, when she entered, she was startled to find that, as Ruth had stated, the room resembled nothing so much as an artist's studio. An easel stood by the window where the morning light would fall. The canvas mounted on it was only partially completed; it was a warm, mellow-colored picture of a woodland scene in which a girl's slim figure knelt by a winding stream. Trees bent above her in a great arc of green, and the reflection in the stream gave back the laughing face of a forest nymph.

Other pictures, in various stages of development, leaned against the walls or were piled in a heap in the corner. It was difficult to conceive of the fact that Lynda had created all of them in such a short time.

"Hi," Kit said. "I brought you some dinner. Madame said that you weren't feeling well."

Lynda was stretched, fully clothed, upon the bed. She was wearing no makeup, and her hair lay oily and matted against the pillow, as though she had not bothered to wash it for a long time.

She glanced at the tray and wrinkled her nose.

"Thanks, but I really don't want anything. I'm not at all hungry."

"You need to eat," Kit said. "You're getting thin."

87

The words were true. Lynda's eyes seemed huge in her pretty face, and the delicate tracery of her high cheekbones stood out beneath the normally perfect skin. Now that skin had a yellowish cast.

"I said, I'm not hungry," Lynda said peevishly. "I'm just tired. I've been working hard."

"I should say you have, from the looks of things." Kit nodded toward the picture on the easel. "That's going to be nice."

"Is it?" Lynda said. "I suppose so."

"What are you going to put over there?" Kit gestured toward an unfinished area in the foreground.

"How should I know? It'll come to me when I get the brush in my hand." Lynda turned her face away and threw an arm across her eyes. "Take that food out of here, will you? I can't stand the smell of it."

Kit regarded her with concern. "I hope you're better tomorrow."

"I will be," Lynda said. "I'll have to be. There's so much to be done. He wants so much. There just isn't any stopping."

"*He?*" Kit caught at the word. "What do you mean? Who is it who wants so much?"

"Please," Lynda said, "just let me be, won't you? I'm so tired. We'll talk another time, okay?"

"Okay." Kit stood a moment longer, gazing down at the slender form on the bed. Was this Lynda Hannah, the bright-faced girl with the lilting laugh, whose sole worry less than two months ago had been the fact that Blackwood would not be sponsoring boy-girl parties? She's changed, Kit thought. Not just a surface change, but all the way down inside. She's not the same person.

"Lynda," she said softly, "please, tell me. Something's happened. Can't you tell me about it?"

The girl on the bed did not answer. Her breathing was

slow and deep, and Kit realized suddenly that she was already asleep.

Natalie was scraping plates when Kit brought the tray back down to the kitchen. She glanced at the untouched plate and shook her head.

"Won't eat, huh?"

"She says she's tired," Kit said.

"Funny," Natalie said. "Nobody's eating the way they used to, except for the gentlemen, maybe, and Madame herself. What's with you girls? All coming down with something?"

"I hope not," Kit said, setting the tray on the counter. She paused, knowing that this was the opportunity for which she had been hoping. "Natalie — can I ask you something?"

"You know I'm not supposed to spend time talking to you young ladies." Natalie was silent a moment, then her curiosity got the better of her. "What is it you want to know?"

"About Blackwood. It's been here a long time, hasn't it? You must have heard a lot of things about it."

"It's an old place, sure," Natalie said. "But Blackwood is the new name for it. It used to be called the old Brewer place. Nobody lived here then. It was all grown over so you could hardly see through the fence, just the roof sticking up."

"How do you know?" Kit asked. "Did you look through the fence and see?"

"Well, we all did," Natalie said, with a note of defensiveness in her voice. "All of us kids, I mean. There were so many stories about it. Teenagers used to come up and park in the driveway."

"Did you?"

"Once or twice," Natalie said, flushing slightly. "Nothing happened. We didn't see anything. I figured the ones who said they did were just making up stories to scare the rest of us."

"What did the others see, or pretend to see?" Kit persisted. "Did they ever tell you?"

"Oh, lights in the windows. Shapes moving around. Things like that. Of course, old man Brewer was supposed to have been pretty strange himself back when he lived here. Anybody who'd live alone in a place this size would have had to have been a little bit off."

"He lived here alone?" Kit exclaimed. "Just one person in this huge place?"

"Well, not in the beginning," Natalie said, running the hot water into the sink and dumping in some detergent. "When he first moved here he had a nice family — a pretty wife, they say, and three or four children. The place was kept up fine then with servants and gardeners, and what Madame Duret has made into an apartment for the professor, that was a real carriage house. Then one night there was a fire. Mr. Brewer was away on a business trip at the time, and they never did find out how it started, but it was in the bedroom wing where the family was sleeping. They had to bring the volunteer fire department up from the village, which took a long time because it was a Saturday night and a lot of the volunteer firemen couldn't be located. By the time they got up here and got the fire under control, it was too late."

"You mean Mr. Brewer's whole family died?" Kit asked in horror. "His wife and all the children?"

"They say it was the smoke that did it," Natalie said. "There wasn't that much damage to the house. When old man Brewer got home and found out what had happened, he got rid of all the servants and barred up the gate. From then on he lived here alone.

"He'd go down to the village for church on Sundays and talk about the family like they were still there, still living in the place with him. Or he'd go to the grocery store and say, 'The missus wants me to pick up some things for her,' and he'd buy candy and stuff for the kids and cereal for the baby."

"That's awful!" Kit gasped. "Just awful! The poor man! How long did this go on?"

"Years and years," Natalie told her. "Talk got started around the town that his family was living here with him, as spirits. Once he called a man to fix the plumbing, and the man said that somewhere in the back of the house he heard a baby crying. After that, he couldn't get people up here to do anything.

"When he died, it was weeks before anybody knew it. Finally they started wondering about his missing church one Sunday after another. So they came up here, and there he was, on one side of the double bed. They say there was a hollow next to him, as though somebody had been lying there."

"After he died," Kit asked, "what happened then?"

"Oh, they got hold of some distant cousins who came in to bury him. They didn't want the place, and after the funeral they listed it with a real estate agency. It was really weathered down when Madame Duret bought it. She's had a lot of work done — the grounds got in shape and the roof repaired — and, of course, she had the sleeping wing fixed up so you girls could live there."

"The sleeping wing," Kit said slowly. An icy shudder went down her spine. "You mean the wing where we're sleeping is where the fire took place?"

"That's right," Natalie said. "But you'd never know it, she's got it remodeled so nice. The help she hired from the village, though, they didn't like cleaning up there. Said it gave them the creeps. That's why they quit."

"Natalie!" A low, strong voice spoke from behind them.

Kit turned quickly to see Madame Duret standing in the kitchen doorway. The woman's face was pale with anger, and her black eyes were blazing.

"Natalie, you had your instructions not to spend your time talking with our students!"

"I'm sorry, ma'am," Natalie said contritely. "I don't do it often."

There was ice in Madame's voice. "Your instructions were not to do it at all."

"It's not Natalie's fault," Kit said. "I'm the one responsible."

Madame's eyes shifted to rest upon her, and Kit felt the power of them touch her with the force of an electric shock. It was as though two needles had thrust themselves through her body.

"You must have homework to do, Kathryn," Madame said. Her voice was like steel. "I would suggest that you go upstairs to your room and get started on it. Natalie is responsible for her own actions. She does not need you to defend her."

"But, she only —" Kit began, and the words faded from her lips under the penetration of that black stare.

She tried to look at Natalie, but she was unable to move her eyes. Against her will, she found herself moving from her position by the kitchen sink.

As though of their own accord her two legs began to carry her step by step across the kitchen and through the door into the dining room.

And into the outer hall.

And up the stairs.

And down the dark, upstairs hallway to her room.

When she closed her eyes the music began. No longer did it hold back until she slept; it seemed now to lie just behind her eyelids, waiting for them to drop, so that as soon as she went into inner darkness the music was there.

With increasing power, it took over the edges of her mind and crept relentlessly toward its core.

I'm dreaming, Kit told herself firmly, but she was not completely sure that this was true. She was too conscious of the pillow beneath her cheek, of the blanket across her shoulders. She knew that she was cold.

If I open my eyes, she thought, it will be gone.

But will it? an inner voice whispered. Are you certain?

Chapter 11

———◆———

Dear Tracy —

This is going to seem like a crazy letter. I wish you were here so I could talk to you directly. You're always so sensible, I'm sure you could come up with an answer — and yet, when I think about it, I can't even tell you the *question*. All I know is that something is very wrong. Sometimes I look at myself in the mirror, and it's like looking at a stranger. The face is the same, except thinner — we all seem to be getting thinner — and there is an odd look to it. It may be the circles under the eyes. Can you believe that — me with circles?

But it's not just physical. We're all of us changing in other ways too. Take Lynda, for instance. She has stopped coming to classes and just stays in her room all day, and half the time she doesn't even come down to meals. Madame Duret has a tray sent up to her, but when it comes back there's hardly any food gone from it. When Lynda *does* come down, once in a great while, she looks like a little white ghost, all skin and bones and big staring eyes. And the eyes don't seem to focus on us. They look through us or past us, as though they are seeing something the rest of us can't.

When you talk to Lynda she answers in this odd, vague way, as if her mind is somewhere else, and sometimes the answers don't go with our questions. There are other times when she doesn't seem to know we're here.

It's just plain scary, and yesterday Ruth went to Madame Duret and suggested that Lynda might need a doctor. Madame said she was sure there was nothing wrong. She said Lynda has just awakened to the discovery of her talent as an artist and is working very hard, and that it's no wonder she is tired, but that it is a good kind of tired, the sort that comes when you really accomplish something.

Is it possible that something "good" can make a person look and act the way Lynda does now?

And then, there's Sandy. She, too, is changing. She dreams a lot, and she tells me that it is always the same dream, the one about the woman who comes and stands by her bed. At first it used to frighten her, but somehow it doesn't seem to anymore. She says the woman's name is Ellis, and she speaks of her as though she were a real person.

Tracy, am I going crazy? For I dream too. In my dreams I am at the piano playing — not the way I usually play, but very well — and there's never any sheet music in front of me. In the beginning the music was always soft and beautiful and the dream was a happy one, but it's not like that anymore. Now the music tears through me with so much power that it is a physical pain. When I wake up, I'm tired. My arms and hands ache as though I had really been playing for hours.

I've found out some background information about Blackwood. I don't like it, any of it. Tracy, I don't want to stay here any longer. I don't care if this is all in my imagination, I still don't want to be here. I've written

Mom and asked her if I can't live with you and your family until she and Dan get home. Would that be all right with your folks? I sure hope so.

Write to me. It's been a long time since I've heard from you, and you never answer any of my questions or comment on any of the things I've written about. Is it possible my letters to you are getting lost in the mail? Or might it be that they aren't getting mailed at all? Professor Farley makes the trip into the village each day and carries our letters to the post office. He *must* mail them — mustn't he? I mean, it would be against the law for him not to, wouldn't it? I'm so confused. Tracy, please, please, write.

"I've written another poem," said Sandy.

"Oh?" Kit did not meet her friends eyes, but she felt her stomach begin to tighten in nervous anticipation.

"I'm not doing this alone," Sandy said. "Ellis is helping me. She's a wonderful writer. She's even published a novel."

"Sandy, please," Kit said wearily. "I wish you'd stop talking about this woman as though she were a real person."

"Listen, now," Sandy said. "See if you like this.

Out of the wind that rules the realm of night
And lonely stars held captive in the sky,
I search for Peace, that death may pass me by
Lost in eternity, as light in light
Is lost, beyond the echo of a Sigh.
Where moonlight on the moors in patterns gleams
Against the shadows, only Peace should be,
And there I search, but peace is not for me.
A moment's rest, left undisturbed by dreams,
Is all I ask —

"Stop! Please, stop!" Kit held up a restraining hand. "I don't want to hear the rest. It's morbid. It sounds as though you're *dead*."

"I thought you'd like it," Sandy said in a hurt voice.

"Well, I don't. What's happened to you, Sandy? We used to laugh so much together. Remember the jokes we used to tell and how we planned to short-sheet Ruth's bed? We were going to have a party one night too, and sneak a lot of food up to my room and make it a midnight feast."

"Do you still want to do those things?" Sandy asked in wonder.

"No," Kit admitted. Somehow the plans that had sounded like so much fun in the early days at Blackwood now seemed childish and ridiculous.

Sandy glanced down at the poem in her hands.

"Ellis doesn't think it's very good," she said. "She doesn't want me to submit it to a publisher or anything. She thinks we can do better —"

"You're doing it again!" Kit interrupted in exasperation. "You're talking about this — this dream person — as though she were real!"

"Is she a dream?" Sandy asked slowly. "When she talks to me, it's so sensible and right. I've been thinking — Kit, do you remember what Ruth was saying about our all having various forms of extrasensory perception?"

Kit nodded.

"Well, what if I've used mine to tune in on somebody, a real person who is living somewhere in the world and has a mind that operates on the same wavelength that mine does. Is that so impossible?"

"You mean you think that somewhere there really is a woman named Ellis?" Kit asked incredulously.

"Why not? She doesn't have to be anywhere near here or even in this country. In fact, I have a feeling she *isn't* in this country — the way she speaks and her references to things like moors and yew trees — she may live someplace like England or Scotland."

"It isn't possible," Kit said. "People don't communicate through dreams. They write letters — they make phone calls —"

"Don't yell," Sandy said. "You're making my head hurt. I can't explain this, Kit. Ruth's the one who's the expert on scientific happenings. All I know is that Ellis is real to me, more real than any dream could be. Whether or not you like her poetry doesn't matter. *I* like it, and I'm happy to be the one to whom she communicates it."

Her narrow face was flushed with anger, and Kit felt her own temper flaring in response.

"You sound like a twelve-year-old who has a crush on a movie star! Except that with a movie star at least you can see her on the screen."

"Oh, shut up," Sandy snapped. "I'm sorry for the day I ever told you about Ellis."

"You didn't have to tell me. I heard you screaming, remember? You didn't think this super poet was so great *then!*" Try as she would, Kit could not bite back the sharp words. "It's this place, this awful place! It's doing something to you! You're getting almost as nutty as Lynda!"

But Sandy had already turned on her heel and left the room, shoving the door shut hard behind her.

Exhausted, Kit let herself fall back across her bed. The intensity of the argument left her drained and vaguely frightened. Sandy was her friend, the closest friend she had in this strange, fenced-in world of Blackwood. How could she possibly have spoken to her in such a way, practically accusing her of being crazy? Why were Sandy's rationalizations any less to be respected than her own or Ruth's? If Sandy was crazy, then they all were.

She should call her back and apologize. She knew it, and yet her weariness was so great that the effort was more than she could make. She raised her hands and pressed them tight against her eyelids, and felt the throbbing in her head which was the beginning of the music.

I won't listen, she told herself. This time I'll defeat it. I won't lie here and listen.

But as had happened that night in the kitchen when Madame Duret had ordered her upstairs, her body would not obey her mental command. It lay upon the bed, and like an audience at a concert, Kit felt the music rushing upon her, soft at first, then louder and stronger, picking up pace and volume.

"Sandy!" she longed to cry. "Sandy — come back! Come help me!"

But although she could feel her throat straining with the words, they were lost in the music. Louder, it came — building and building to what she knew would soon be a crashing crescendo.

Too tired to combat it, she stopped resisting and let herself go, to be carried like a leaf in a rushing current of silent sound.

Eventually she slept. She was not conscious of this happening, but when she opened her eyes the afternoon light had faded from the sky beyond the window and the room was dark.

And there was cold. So much cold that she did not know if she could move. Her whole body was leaden with the weight of it. It was the same strange cold that she had felt in Sandy's room on that night so many weeks ago, a chill too intense to be natural, touched with the feel of dampness and a faint odor which she could not place.

For a few moments she lay there, unmoving. Then, with a gigantic effort, she stretched out her hand and found the lamp. The light sprang on, and the familiar room came into being around her — the bureau, the desk, the gilt-edged mirror, the arched red canopy over the bed.

Fighting the lethargy that threatened to drag her back into unconsciousness, Kit got up and went to the closet for a sweater. Taking it from its hanger, she thrust her arms into the sleeves and buttoned it up to the neck. The cold seemed to slide through the heavy material and seep into her very pores.

Shivering violently, she glanced at her watch. Six forty-five. Downstairs in the dining room dinner would be underway. She could picture the great round table under the twinkling chandelier and the group that would be gathered around it — Madame, stately and gracious; friendly, bearded Professor Farley; Jules, handsome and brooding. Ruth would be at the table. And Sandy.

I'd better go down, Kit thought, if only to see Sandy. If I don't, she'll think it's because of our argument. The sooner things could be made right between herself and Sandy the better.

The thought of food made her feel slightly nauseated. Still, anything was better than staying alone in a room that was as cold as a tomb.

Stepping out into the hall, Kit pulled the door closed behind her and locked it. The air was warmer here, but she still found herself shivering. At the far end of the hall the dim bulb threw out its faint circle of light, and the whole corridor seemed made out of shadows.

Slowly, Kit began to walk down the hallway toward the stairs. In the mirror at the hall's end she saw a thin, white-faced girl in a heavy-knit sweater moving toward her.

Is that me? she thought, momentarily startled by the girl's appearance, the dullness of the eyes, the limp, uncombed hair, the heavy, methodical walk. Was this the same Kit Gordy who had bounced down this hallway only a matter of months ago, eyes shining, face alight, to greet her new classmates?

I look awful, Kit thought wretchedly. Just awful.

And then, as she tilted her head, she caught sight of him, the person walking behind her.

In horror she stood there, frozen, one foot lifted for the next step, her eyes staring into the other eyes reflected in the mirror.

It can't be, she told herself. There can't be anyone behind me. The hall was vacant when I came out of my room. Anyone behind me now would have had to have come out of it with me, and that's impossible.

And yet the man was there, his image as clear as her own, standing so close behind her that it was incredible that she did not feel his breath upon the back of her neck.

Dragging in her breath, Kit did the only thing that she could do. She closed her eyes and screamed.

Chapter 12

———◆———

Once she started, she could not stop. Scream after scream tore from her throat in great, ragged shrieks. For what seemed a million years she screamed, until as though from another world she heard the sound of footsteps pounding on the stairs and a voice calling her name.

Strong hands closed upon her shoulders.

Jules's voice said, "Kit! Kit, what is it? My Lord, what's happened?"

"There —" Kit managed to sob, "there — behind me —"

"There's nothing behind you."

Kit opened her eyes and stared up at him, at the fine-boned, perfectly featured face bent close to her own, at the heavy-lidded dark eyes, filled now with real concern. Gone was the anger that had flared there the day she had intruded upon him in the music room while he was playing the Schubert tape. Gone was the discomfort that had existed between them since.

He cares, she thought, And even through her terror she clutched at the realization. He does care.

"There was someone," she said chokingly. "A man.

He was walking behind me. I saw him reflected in the mirror."

"There can't have been."

"There *was!*"

"There, now — you're okay. It's all right." Jules pulled her against him so that her face was buried against his shirtfront, and his hand ran lightly over her hair. "You saw a shadow. Or perhaps it was your own reflection."

"It was a man!" She tried to cry the words, but they were muffled by the warm bulk of his shoulder.

From somewhere beyond them she heard other voices and she knew that they were coming, all of them, from the floor below. In another moment they would be here surrounding her, patting and comforting her, telling her in rational terms what it was that she had been imagining.

Pressing her hands against Jules's chest, she shoved him away from her so that she could see his face.

"Please," she said frantically, "you must believe me. You have to believe me."

"Kathryn!" The voice was Madame Duret's. "What in the world has occurred?"

"What is it, Kit?"

"Kit, are you all right?"

"Was that *you* we heard?"

She had known it would be this way. Professor Farley, Ruth, Sandy — all of them worried. She felt Sandy's hand touch her arm, a silent reassurance that their friendship was still intact. If no one else did, Sandy would believe her.

"She's frightened," Jules explained. "She thought she saw somebody in the mirror."

"Somebody?"

"A man. I saw a man." Kit struggled to get control of

her voice. "I didn't just think I saw him, I *did* see him. He was just as real as I am."

"What did he look like?" Professor Farley asked her. His keen, old eyes were regarding her intently.

"I — don't know," Kit said haltingly. "The hall's so dark, I couldn't see him well. And my own reflection was partially blocking him. But he was there. There's no doubt about it."

"Then where has he gone?" Madame Duret asked matter-of-factly. She gestured toward the stretch of empty hallway leading back to Kit's door. "If someone had been there, chérie, he would have to be there still. If he had run past you, he would have had to pass us on the stairs."

"He could have gone back," Sandy suggested timidly. She dropped her hand and slipped it into Kit's. "Kit's room and mine are both down at that end of the hall. He might have gone into one of them."

"You keep your rooms locked, don't you?" Ruth asked. She sounded more interested than worried. Her eyes were aglitter with subdued excitement.

"Yes, but still —"

Kit could tell from Ruth's face that she too was remembering the instance of the missing portrait when a locked door had been no deterrent to an invader. She knows something, she thought. Somehow Ruth has gone a step ahead of the rest of us.

"Well, there's one way to be sure of things," said Professor Farley. "Give me your keys, girls, and Jules and I will check your rooms. If there's any possible chance that there is someone in this building who doesn't belong here, we want to know about it."

Sandy and Kit both handed him their keys. In silence they watched the two men go down the hall and enter first one room and then the other.

It did not take long.

"All empty," Professor Farley said. "There's nobody in the closets or under the beds. I'm afraid you were imagining things, young lady. I can see how one might, too, the way the shadows shift about. Walking toward the mirror gives one a strange sensation."

"But I wasn't imagining," Kit exclaimed. And then, a bit doubtfully, "He seemed so real."

"Like my Ellis?" Sandy suggested softly.

"No," Kit said. "Not like that. I was wide awake, not dreaming."

"Are you sure?"

"Of course I'm sure. I was standing right here."

"I think we had best return to the dining room," Madame Duret said firmly. The tone of her voice, pleasant but definite, told them that the issue was now behind them, something that need not be agonized over or discussed any further. "The professor is correct, the light in this hallway is terribly disconcerting. I shall call once again tomorrow about those electricians, and if I cannot get someone from the village, I will call into Middleton.

"Now, do let us return to our dinner before everything is cold. Are you feeling better, Kathryn?"

"Yes, ma'am," Kit said shakily. And though the last thing she felt like doing was eating, she let herself be guided down the stairs and on into the dining room.

The table had been cleared of the soup bowls. They took their seats, and at the tinkle of Madame's silver bell the kitchen door opened and Lola appeared, her gray brows drawn together in a scowl.

"Please to bring the main course now," Madame told her.

Without a word the older women turned and went back through the doorway. Kit stared after her in bewilderment.

"Why is Lola doing the serving?" she asked. "Is Natalie sick?"

"Natalie is no longer in my employment," Madame informed her. Her voice carried no hint of emotion, but Kit, remembering the scene in the kitchen when those two black eyes had struck her like thunderbolts, was filled with a sudden dread suspicion.

"Why?" she asked. "Did you — let her go?"

"Let her go? Why, of course not." Madame took her napkin and spread it in her lap. "Good cooks like Natalie are difficult to acquire these days. No, the girl asked to leave. She is to be married a week from Saturday."

"Married!" Kit exclaimed. It was the last thing she had expected to be told.

"How nice," Ruth commented. "She will probably make somebody a very good wife. Who is she marrying, somebody from the village?"

"I imagine so. Whom else would she find?" Madame said easily. "But with so much of our help gone now, I am afraid we shall all have to do a bit of the work. Nice as it would be, a place like Blackwood does not take care of itself, you know. Starting tomorrow, I must make out a chore list for everyone."

The door swung open again and Lola entered, bearing a platter of overdone chops, and the subject of conversation was terminated.

The phone call came at eight-thirty that evening. The girls were gathered in the parlor watching television when Jules appeared suddenly in the doorway.

"Phone for you, Kit," he said. "Long distance. Your mother."

"It is!" For a moment Kit thought her heart would leap out of her chest. In an instant she was on her feet, hurrying toward him. "Where can I take it?"

"The only phone is in the office," Jules said. "You'd better hurry. Overseas calls cost a mint."

When she entered the office, Kit found Madame Duret seated at her desk. The telephone sat at her right, the receiver off the hook. Madame picked it up and held it out to Kit.

"Are you not the lucky one — a call from Italy! Do give your mother my regards."

Kit snatched for the receiver. She found her hand was trembling as she raised it to her ear.

"Hello — Mom?"

"Oh, honey!" Her mother's tiny voice sounded a million miles away, but the warmth, the inflections, the love, were so familiar that for the second time that evening Kit found her eyes blurred with tears. "It's so wonderful to hear you."

"You too," Kit said. "How are you? How's Dan? Where are you calling from? Are you having fun?"

"So much fun," her mother said, "you can't imagine. We're in Florence now, and tomorrow we leave for Rome. Just think, we'll actually be visiting St. Peter's and the Forum and the Catacombs — all the places you always read about!"

She sounds so young, Kit thought in amazement.

Her mother, with the silver threads in her hair, the soft cobweb of lines at the corners of her eyes, the back that ached after a day of typing, sounded like a young girl, bubbling with enthusiasm and vitality.

"And you, honey? How are you? Do you love it at Blackwood?"

"Mother!" Kit was stunned at the question. "Haven't you been reading my letters?"

"We got one in Cherbourg," her mother said, "but that was almost immediately after we arrived. It's the

107

only letter we've received. That's why I'm calling. Dan said he was sure that you were just too busy to write, but I was worried that you might be ill. You haven't been, have you?"

"No," Kit said. "And I've written every week. I've told you about everything — absolutely everything."

In her chair at the desk, Madame shifted her weight, and Kit moved a few paces away, stretching the telephone cord to its full length.

"It's the mails then," Kit's mother said. "It's so hard to be sure of your timing when you're sending things care of American Express. You must be just missing us every place we go. Well, tell me, how is everything? Are you studying hard? Do you have nice friends?"

"I — I —" Kit could not get an answer out. Instead she said, "Mother, how much longer are you going to stay over there? When are you coming home?"

"The week before Christmas," her mother said. "Don't you remember the plan? We'll coincide with your vacation."

"But, that's months away!" The words burst from her in a strangled cry. "I can't stay here that long, Mom, I just can't! You don't know — you don't understand!"

Madame Duret moved in her chair. Kit felt the intense black eyes boring into her, and she clutched the receiver more tightly against her ear.

"Oh, honey!" There was mild exasperation in her mother's voice. "Are you still upset with us for coming to Europe without you? I thought you'd accepted the situation. You told me —"

"It's not that, really! I swear, that has nothing to do with it. I want to tell you — please, you have to listen —"

There was so much to tell, all the things that she had poured out in her letters and assumed her mother knew, and now realized that she did not know at all. But where could she start? The beginning seemed so long ago, and there was so much — Lynda and her art, Sandy, the dreams, the music, the man in the hall, whom she was sure, really sure, she had not imagined, and yet what other explanation could there be? And her mother was so far away, just a thin, small voice on the other end of a transatlantic cable, with the minutes piling up, each one costing a small fortune.

But most of all there was Madame Duret, seated here beside her, listening to every word that she spoke. Those eyes — those impossible eyes — rested upon her face, and she could not turn from them, could not focus her own gaze anywhere except into their depths. They held her still, impaled, like a bug on two sharp pins.

"Mother —" she said, and she could not go on.

"I think that this conversation must be costing your mother a great deal of money, Kathryn." Madame spoke quietly, but her voice held a note of command. "Do you not think that you should give her your love and say goodbye?"

"Mom!" Kit made one final desperate effort. "I want to stay at Tracy's. Can't I, please? I've written her, and it will be all right, I know it will. I could get the bus in Blackwood Village — Mr. Rosenblum could meet me — and I could stay with them until Christmas, until you and Dan got home —"

"Oh, Kit, really!" The lilting youthfulness was gone from her mother's voice. In its place was a blend of disappointment, concern and weariness. "You'll be seeing Tracy at Christmastime. No matter what you say, it really isn't very far away. Enjoy your other friends now, the new ones you've made at Blackwood. In your one letter you mentioned a girl named Sandy. You seemed to like her. Don't you still?"

"Yes. Yes, sure, I like Sandy."

What shall I do? Kit asked herself frantically. What *can* I do? She looked down into Madame Duret's face, and no further words would come.

"Do write, honey," her mother was saying. "And aim your letters a little further ahead. You have our itinerary. Allow a few extra days for them to reach us, and for goodness sake, don't forget to use airmail. Dan sends his love. He's a fine man, Kit — a good, kind person. I realize it more each day. I'm very lucky."

"Yes," Kit said resignedly. "Yes, I know."

"I love you, honey."

"I love you too." The time was up. There was no way, no possible way. "Tell Dan hello. Have a happy honeymoon."

"We will. You too — be happy, honey. Good-bye for now."

"Good-bye." There was a little click and silence.

Kit lowered the receiver from her ear and placed it carefully back upon the hook. She closed her eyes so that she would not have to see the look of satisfaction on Madame's face, but she could not keep them closed. One could not stand for very long with one's eyes screwed shut.

"That is right, chérie," Madame Duret told her. "You want to leave your mother enough money to purchase some gifts to bring back with her. Are they having a pleasant trip?"

"Yes," Kit said dully. "A wonderful time."

"They seemed so nice, both of them. You would not wish to ruin their trip by having them concerned about you. All girls become a bit homesick on occasion. It is one of those things one must fight against."

"I suppose," Kit said.

Miserably, she turned and started across the room to

the door, and stopped short as her eyes fell upon a painting on the opposite wall over a filing cabinet. A mountain lake reflected light from the sky — green woods, distant hills. The familiarity of the setting struck her like a well-known cry.

"What's that?" she asked.

"That cabinet? It is where I keep my files on former students."

"I didn't mean the cabinet," Kit said. "I meant the picture. Who did it?"

"Do you like the painting? It is a favorite of mine." It was as though there had been no contest between them. "It is a landscape by Thomas Cole. A reproduction, of course."

"I've seen that lake," Kit said.

"Perhaps you have. The picture was painted in the Catskills."

"No, I mean I've seen it painted before. From another angle." Kit continued to stare at the landscape. "There's a footpath over there along the shore, but you can't see it from this direction."

Then the realization struck her.

"It's the same lake that has been in some of Lynda's paintings."

"Why, I do not think so, chérie," Madame Duret said. "Lynda comes from California. I hardly think she would be painting New York scenery."

"But, it is. I know it is," Kit insisted. "Who is this Thomas Cole, anyway? Does he live around here?"

"He did at one time," Madame Duret told her. "Of course, that was many years ago. He died in the middle of the nineteenth century."

Chapter 13

———◆———

"It's true," Ruth said. "Thomas Cole was a really famous artist. I'm surprised you haven't heard of him. He was the founder of the Hudson River School of landscape painters."

It was late afternoon of the following day, and they had left the house to walk around to the far side of the pond. It was a gray and winterish day, quite different from the bright autumn weather that they had been having, and Kit felt it as an echo of her own spirits. She thrust her hands deep into the pockets of her jeans and stared across at the dead brown stalks that were all that was left of the summer garden.

"And he's dead?" she asked.

"Oh, sure. Ages ago. He died comparatively young too. He was only in his forties. He was one of a batch of American artists we studied in one of the enrichment classes at the last school I went to."

"You learned about him there?" Kit drew a breath of relief. "And Lynda too?"

"No, not Lynda," Ruth said. "She didn't take the enrichment courses. Why is it you're suddenly so hung up on Thomas Cole?"

Kit's head was aching. It seemed to her lately that her head was always throbbing with a dull pressure. Sometimes it was because of the music inside it, ringing and crashing and filling her ears with sounds that no one else could hear.

Other times, like now, the pressure was a thing unto itself, an ache that seemed born of confusion and fatigue.

"I'm so mixed up," she said. "I hardly know where to begin thinking. Nothing makes any sense."

"What's happened?" Ruth asked. "It must be something important if you wanted to come all the way out here to talk about it."

"It was last night," Kit said. "When I was in Madame's office, taking the phone call from my mother. On the wall over a filing cabinet, there was a reproduction of a painting of a lake. Madame said it was by Thomas Cole."

"So?"

"It was the same lake that Lynda paints, and more than that, it looked exactly like one of Lynda's landscapes. The lighting, the colors, the sky — all of it. Lynda might have done it herself."

"That's why you asked if she had studied Thomas Cole?"

"If she had, it would have at least partially explained things. She might have been imitating his work, don't you think? Unconsciously — not even realizing what she was doing? But if she didn't take the course with you, then that's out. There has to be some other answer."

"T.C.," Ruth said softly.

"What?"

"Those are the initials — T.C. It's the way Lynda signs her paintings."

"T.C. — for Thomas Cole?" Kit turned to her incredulously. "Then she must know who he is — she *has* to! She must have seen his work somewhere, perhaps on some television special. And she admires him. She's trying so hard to imitate him that she's using his initials to — well, to sort of bring herself luck."

"No," Ruth said. "I can't buy that. Sorry. I wish it were true, but I'm sure it isn't."

A breeze touched the surface of the pond, making little ripples, and the trees reflected in its surface shimmered and shifted like live creatures in the moving water. Across the pond, the roof of Blackwood rose sharp against the heavy overcast of the sky. The windows stared out at them like empty eyes.

The kitchen door opened suddenly and Lola came out with a bag of trash for the incinerator. Her grayness seemed part of the day itself.

"*She'll* never quit, at least," Ruth commented. "I bet she's been with Madame since the very beginning."

"Natalie didn't quit," Kit said. "She was fired."

"Madame said she quit."

"I know, but I don't believe it. Natalie needed her job, and if she had a boyfriend, she never bothered to mention him. I'm sure she would have if she had been serious enough to consider getting married."

"But why would Madame have let her go?" Ruth asked. "Lola can't cook. That chicken last night was so greasy I could hardly swallow it. Natalie's meals were the best part of the day."

"Natalie talked," Kit said. "Remember how I was going to ask her about the background of Blackwood? Well, Madame Duret walked in on us while she was telling me, and she was furious. I'm sure that after I left she fired Natalie."

"Then she *did* tell you about it?" Ruth was more interested in this fact than in the fate of Natalie. "What did you find out?"

"Some terrible things. Mr. Brewer's whole family was killed in a fire, and he went off his rocker. He wouldn't admit that they were gone. He lived the whole rest of his life here just as though they were still alive, talking about them and buying toys for the children and everything."

"Did Mr. Brewer die in the house too?"

"Yes," Kit said. "A long time later. Why do you ask that? Ruth —" She stopped at the look on the girl's face. Something was flickering there, a glint of revelation. "Ruth, what is it? Do you know something that I don't?"

"I don't *know* anything," Ruth said. "Anything I came up with right now would just be a guess."

"But you have an idea?"

"It's way-out," Ruth said. "So far out that I don't think you'd accept it. I don't know that I can accept it myself."

"What is it?"

"I don't want to talk about it right now," Ruth said. "I want to think about it a while first. Did you say the woman in Sandy's dream is named Ellis and she comes from England?"

"That's what Sandy has decided. Either there or Scotland, someplace with moors."

"Did she ever mention the woman's last name?"

"No."

"I'm going to check something out in the library," Ruth said. "If it turns out my guess is right, then I'll tell you about it. But you'd better prepare yourself. If I *have* found the answer, you're going to get the shock of your life."

That night, as always, there was the music. Soft, this

time, like a lullaby for a child. Moonlight on a pillow. Tree limbs rustling outside a window in the faint evening breeze. Fireflies on the lawn. Soft laughter from couples sitting on the porch steps.

I am asleep, Kit told herself. I know that I am asleep, lying in the bed with the canopy over it, and the room is dark and still, and this music is not real. It is a dream, only a dream. When I wake, it will be morning with breakfast waiting in the dining room down below and classes to go to, and the music will be gone again as though it has never been.

A voice spoke softly, breaking through the music. A man's voice, gruff, but oddly gentle.

"Gone, for a moment. But not really. Never really gone."

Because she knew it was a dream, Kit was not startled.

"Who are you?" she asked. And then she recognized him, and her heart gave a lurch. "I've seen you before. You were the one standing behind me in the hall, the one I saw in the mirror."

"Of course," the dream man said. He seemed surprised that *she* should be surprised.

"Why were you following me?" Kit asked. "Why are you here now? What is it you want?"

"I am here to give."

"That's no answer."

"It's the only answer," the man said patiently. "You are one of the fortunate ones who are blessed with the ability to receive."

"To receive — what?" Kit asked. And then the answer came to her and she began to understand. "The music? Are you the one who is sending me this music, the way Ellis is sending Sandy poetry? If you are, you must take it back. I don't want it — any of it."

116

The sounds rose within her, louder now, changing pace and rhythm, beginning to leap and build as they did so often lately into a pressure that swelled her brain.

This is a dream, she reminded herself frantically. Only a dream.

"Of course, it is," the man said and reached for her hand. His fingers closed around her wrist, and it was all that she could do to keep from crying out at the icy touch as he drew her from the bed. She felt the carpet beneath her bare feet and saw him reach for the knob of the door.

"Where are you taking me?"

"You must let it out," the man said.

"Let what out? What do you mean?"

They were in the hall now, and he was leading her down it through the darkness with the assurance of one who knows each step, while the music grew louder and louder, pounding against the inside of her skull.

"You must let it out, or your head will burst with it! You must let it go!"

"How?" Kit sobbed. "How?" She could no longer keep track of where they were going. She knew they were on the stairs — she could feel cold floorboards against the soles of her feet — doors opened and closed. There were other voices, a muted chorus of voices, but the music overwhelmed them.

"Here she is," the dream man said. "I've brought her down."

"It will be my turn now," someone said. "I haven't used her yet."

"No, mine! She must play for me!"

"I want her tonight! She was yours last time — she did that concerto —"

"You forget — I brought her down!"

Kit felt a keyboard beneath her fingers.

117

"But, I don't know how to play!"

And even as she cried the words she was playing, and it was the old, old dream, with her hands leaping upon the ivory keys and the great thunderous chords rolling forth.

I am dreaming, Kit told herself for one final time. I am — I am — and I must wake up! I *will* wake myself up!

"No," cried the voice of the man in her dream. "You can't — you mustn't —"

"I will!" She turned upon him with every bit of the strength that she possessed, with all the temper and stubbornness which were the mark of Kathryn Gordy — "*I will!*"

The music was gone.

She was seated on a bench in front of a piano, and she was cold — achingly cold. Blinking, she glanced about her and realized that she was in the music room at Blackwood and that she was not alone.

Across from her, at the tape recorder, sat Jules. The tape was moving, and she realized incredulously that he was recording.

"Jules?" She spoke his name sharply.

With a startled movement he reached out and flicked a switch to halt the machine.

"Jules," Kit said shakily, "what am I doing here?"

"You — you walked in your sleep," Jules said haltingly.

"And you were here to record me? You *were* recording me, weren't you? It's my playing that you have on that tape?"

Wordlessly, Jules nodded. His face was pale, and he looked as though he did not know how to combat the question.

"You've done this before, haven't you?" Kit asked.

"Other nights — I've come down here and played for you. That's what that tape was I heard you playing the other day. It was a recording of me."

"Yes," Jules said. "Look, Kit, I know this must seem awfully strange to you, but believe me, it's nothing to be upset about. Nothing bad has happened. You've always gotten back to your room safely. The only result is that we have the tapes."

"We? Who is 'we'?"

"Well — all of us. The school."

"Your mother? Professor Farley?"

"Don't look that way, Kit. Nobody's done anything to hurt you. Nothing but good has been happening here. We're giving beautiful music to the world."

"It's not my music," Kit said. "I'm no composer. Where is it coming from? Whose is it?" She watched his face close in, and she could see him struggling to think of an answer. "Don't make something up. I want to know the truth. You owe me that, Jules. Tell me — whose music have I been playing?"

"I don't know," Jules stammered. "This time I — well, I just can't tell."

"And other times?"

"I think — I'm almost sure — that for a while at least, it was Franz Schubert."

"Schubert!" Kit exclaimed. "But he died over a century ago!"

"He died in 1828," Jules said. "He was thirty-one years old. He left so much undone, Kit, so many marvelous pieces of music unwritten. His death was a tragic waste of talent."

"And I've been playing his music? I, who can't even get through 'Dancing Leaves' without mistakes?" Kit's voice was shaking. "And there's the rest — Sandy and the poetry, Lynda —" The parts of the puzzle began to move into place, and the thing that was forming in her mind was too incredible to believe.

"Get them," she said quietly. "All of them — Sandy and Lynda and Ruth, the professor, your mother. I want everybody down here right now. I want to know exactly what has been happening here at Blackwood, the whole story!"

"Now, Kit, look," Jules said desperately. "You're all upset, and I don't blame you. But this isn't the time to talk about anything. It's two o'clock in the morning. Everybody's sound asleep. You don't want to bring them all down here now."

Straightening on the bench, Kit glared at him, as anger swept in to take the place of fear. "If you don't get them, Jules, I will. I'll start yelling and I'll bring the whole house awake. I want to know the answer to the mystery of Blackwood, and I don't intend to wait until morning to get it."

Chapter 14

———

"It is two o'clock in the morning, scarcely an hour to hold a conference." Madame Duret's voice was crisp and cold. "I must say, Jules, that you are not showing the best of judgment."

"I couldn't help it," Jules said. "Kit woke up while she was at the piano. Of course, she started asking questions."

"But to bring down everyone!"

Madame was wearing a crimson dressing gown. Her long, black hair, loosed from its usual coil, hung down her back in a great cascade, and her face, void of makeup, had an almost skeletal look in the lamplight.

"I made him," Kit said. "Whatever it is that is happening here involves all of us. I don't care what time of night it is."

She spoke with a firmness that surprised her, and she could see a flicker of grudging respect in Madame's eyes.

"And you?" Madame's gesture took in the other three girls who, in robes and slippers, were now gathered in the parlor. Professor Farley, wearing an overcoat over his pajamas, was seated in an armchair by the window. "You wish this — this confrontation?"

Ruth nodded quickly. Her face was flushed with excitement.

Sandy hesitated, her eyes wide and frightened. Then she nodded also.

Lynda glanced blankly at Ruth.

"What is it she's talking about?" she asked. "Why are we all down here?"

Ruth turned back to Madame Duret. "She has to hear it too. She may not understand, but you'll have to tell her. It's only right."

"Very well," Madame said. "I had planned, of course, to disclose everything in good time, just as I did with the girls in my former schools. I had hoped it could wait a bit longer, however. We are still so close to the beginning. There is so much distance still to be covered before your relationships are secure."

"What relationships?" Kit asked. "With whom?"

Madame did not answer immediately. Instead, she turned to gaze past them, out the window into the darkness that lay beyond the pane.

When she did begin to speak at last, it was slowly, as though she were searching for the perfect words.

"Most people in this world are like children. Their lives run on one level only, the physical level of the here and now. From day to day they go, seeing the material things that surround them, believing that there is nothing beyond this.

"But they are not correct. There is a second level of reality, a spiritual level that is as real as the physical. It transcends the first level and exists beyond it. A few special people are blessed with an extraordinary sensitivity to this spirit world and can bridge with their minds the space between these two realities. I" — a note of pride crept into her voice — "I am one of those people."

Kit stared at her. "Do you mean to say that you're a — a — *medium?*"

"I find that word offensive," Madame said stiffly. "It carries with it a flavor of fakery and parlor tricks. I do not lend myself to such demonstrations. I believe my gift is too valuable to be abused in such ways. It must be used only for the good of humanity."

"Which is how?" Kit asked.

Madame continued as though she had not heard the question.

"Today the average lifetime is over seventy years, long enough for a great number of accomplishments. But this development has occurred within the present century. Before that, people tended to die much younger than they do today, and among those early deaths were those of many brilliant and talented people who had much to give the world. It is to these people whom I reach out. It is to them I offer the opportunity to return."

"To return!" It was Sandy who spoke now, her voice expressionless with shock. "But people can't come back once they're dead!"

"Not in physical form," Madame said. "But in spiritual form, they can, if there is a place for them. By this, I mean that there must be a receiver, a young, clear mind, still uncluttered by worldly problems, impressionable and sensitively tuned. Such minds are unusual, but they do exist. They can be found."

"And you found them in us." Ruth made the statement in a matter-of-fact manner. She did not look or sound surprised. "Through those entrance tests, you were able to tell."

Madame nodded. "My tests took years to develop, and they are dependable. Here at Blackwood, I was fortunate in finding a place of perfect atmosphere. There have been spirit occupants here before. Mr. Brewer was in his own way a medium of a sort. He was able to recall and surround himself with the spirits of his deceased family. Their vibrations remain here still, a part of the house. The trip to Blackwood from the plane beyond is a short one, made along a well-traveled path."

The parts of the puzzle were in place now, but Kit could not believe them. I'm going to be sick, she thought, right here on the parlor floor.

But she wasn't. Instead she simply sat there, staring at the tall, red-gowned woman in growing horror. Could they be true — the things that Madame was saying — could they possibly be true?

"I told you," Ruth said, "that you wouldn't be able to accept it."

Kit turned to her in amazement.

"You already knew?"

"I guessed," Ruth said. "Remember, yesterday, when we were walking by the pond, and I told you I wanted to check something out?"

"Yes."

"Well, I did," Ruth said. "Tonight after dinner I went into the library and looked up a few people. One of them was a woman named Emily Brontë who wrote under the name of Ellis Bell."

"Who?" Sandy asked.

"Emily Brontë — you'll know her best as the author of *Wuthering Heights*. She lived in England during the nineteenth century. It was a time when woman writers were not taken seriously, so she and her two sisters decided to write under masculine pen names."

"Ellis — my Ellis — is *Emily Brontë!*" Sandy shook her head. "That's impossible. Emily Brontë has been dead for years."

"She died in 1848," Ruth said. "Of consumption."

"I don't believe it!" Sandy's voice rose hysterically. "Ellis is just as alive as I am. She writes poetry —"

"She dictates poetry," Ruth corrected, "and you write it down for her. You've admitted yourself that those poems don't come out of your own head. She's using you, Sandy, to get onto paper the words she didn't have time to write while she was alive." She turned to Madame. "Isn't that right?"

Madame nodded.

"Control yourself, Sandra. There is nothing for you to become so upset about."

"Nothing to become upset about!" Sandy cried. "With dead people walking through my mind!"

"You haven't been hurt, my child." From his chair in the corner, Professor Farley spoke for the first time. "You have simply been part of a unique experiment. You should feel privileged, not exploited."

"That's what I've been trying to explain to Kit," Jules said.

"Privileged!" Kit exploded. "By having my mind used as a receiving unit?" She turned accusingly to Professor Farley. "And, you — you're in on this also?"

"Of course," the professor said. His kindly old face held no trace of guilt. "I became acquainted with Madame Duret in London while doing research for a paper on psychic phenomena. When I learned about her school in Paris, I was fascinated. I encouraged her to open another, similar institution in England, and later I accompanied her to America to assist with the establishment of Blackwood."

"I think," Kit said, "that it's the most terrible thing I've ever heard of."

"What's so terrible about it?" Jules asked her. "You ought to be proud."

"Proud of what? That I'm being used, like a tool of some kind?" Kit exclaimed incredulously. The voices from the dream came back to her, and she shuddered uncontrollably. " 'She must play for me!' 'I want her tonight!' 'I haven't used her yet!' It's the way you talk about an object, not a person!"

Lynda was looking dazedly from one speaker to another.

"What is all this?" she asked in bewilderment. "Who's an object?"

"You are!" Kit cried. "We all are! Don't you understand at all, Lynda? It's not you who is doing those beautiful pictures we're so impressed by! It's a famous landscape painter who died over a century ago. No wonder they're so good!"

"That's not true," Lynda said. "I painted all day today. Look — I can prove it." She held out a slim, delicate hand smudged with green paint. "That's from doing the grass. There's a lot of grass in my new picture."

"And who wants it there — that grass? Who planned the picture? Who guides the brush?"

"I don't know what you mean."

"The other evening in your room," Kit said in exasperation, "when I brought up your tray, you said, 'There is so much to be done. *He* wants so much.' Who were you talking about, Lynda? Who is this 'he'?"

"I never said anything like that," Lynda said with a catch in her voice. "I think all you girls are horrid. First Ruth says I'm tracing, and now you say that somebody else is doing the work for me. You're jealous, that's what! Here's the first thing I've ever really been good at in my whole life, and you can't bear to see me get the credit for it."

"Let her be, Kit," Ruth said. "She can't take it in. Can

you blame her? It's an incredible concept. It will take some getting used to for all of us."

"Well, you can get used to it if you want to. Personally, I don't intend to!" Kit turned to Madame Duret. "I'm going home!"

"You cannot do that. Your parents are away."

"I'll stay with friends! The Rosenblums will have me! I'll call Tracy tonight. Her parents will be here by morning. They're that kind of people."

"And they can drop me at the bus stop in the village." Sandy moved to stand beside Kit. "I'm not going to stay in this place a minute longer than I have to. And you'd just better wait until my grandpa hears about this, he'll blow a fuse!"

"Girls, you are being ridiculous." There was a cold edge to Madame's voice. "You cannot back out at this point. The connections are still in the process of being stabilized."

"That's great," Kit said. "I'll break them off before they *do* become stabilized. I'm getting out of here while my brain is still my own. If you think I'm going to sit here and let some wandering spirits take possession of it, you're out of your mind!"

"That is sufficient, Kathryn," Madame said icily. "I ask you to remember, please, that you are a young lady and you will mind your manners accordingly. I do not enjoy listening to yelling, particularly in the middle of the night. It is you who demanded this explanation, and you have now had it, and as far as I am concerned, the discussion is over. You will all please return to your beds. You need your rest in order to be alert for your morning classes."

"I'm not going to be here for classes," Kit told her

127

angrily. "By tomorrow I'll be with the Rosenblums on the way back to the city!"

And then, she stopped as the realization came to her — there was only one telephone at Blackwood. It was located in Madame Duret's private office.

Chapter 15

———————◆———————

The next days moved past in a blur. Nightmare days was the way Kit thought of them. The last of October became the beginning of November, and the final leaves drifted from the branches of the trees around the pond, leaving them stark and bare against the heavy gray of the overcast sky.

Outside the air was damp and chill with the promise of winter, and within the walls of Blackwood a different sort of chill prevailed. Even in the daytime, the house seemed filled with shadows, and in the evenings the girls gathered in the parlor to share the bright reality of the color television set with a sense of relief at finding the banal programs still the same.

"It's as though *this* is the true world," Sandy said thinly, gesturing toward the screen on which a rubber-faced comedienne was imitating a famous opera singer, "and we are the make-believe. Sometimes I wonder if I'm real at all."

"You're real, all right," Kit told her. "We all are. But for how long? We've got to get out of this place as soon as possible."

"How?" Sandy asked hopelessly. "We can't get to the telephone. Madame keeps the office locked at all times. The gate at the end of the drive is padlocked, and there's no way of getting over the fence. I know because I went down to check. Those spikes on top aren't decorations, they're for real."

"I think you're making too much of this," Ruth interjected. She reached over to turn down the volume of the set so that they could talk more easily. "We'll be going home at Christmas. That's not very far off. In the meantime, how many people our age ever get to be intricate parts of such an original experiment?"

"Honestly, Ruth," Sandy said in amazement, "I actually think you're enjoying this. You don't seem to be upset by it at all."

"I was in the beginning," Ruth said, "before I understood what was happening, but now — well, I guess I'm more excited than anything. Imagine having an opportunity to be in on something so significant! It's a true breakthrough in science. And the insight it's giving me is incredible. I have a grasp of mathematical concepts that I never would have believed possible."

"But, it's not you who's grasping them," Kit objected. "It's somebody else, working through your mind!"

"Not entirely," Ruth said. "That's the difference between our situations. You feel that you're being used as a vehicle. You don't have any understanding of the music that's coming through you. You simply 'land' it, mechanically, the way Sandy does her poetry. But in my case, I *am* able, just barely, to begin to get the meaning of the knowledge that is coming through me. Math and science are my thing — they always have been. I feel now as though I have been sitting all my life inside a box, and suddenly someone is lifting the lid and I can look up and see the stars."

"Then there's no actual personality coming into your consciousness?" Kit asked her. "The way there is with Sandy and me?"

"Not that I'm aware of," Ruth told her. "I think perhaps what I'm receiving is a pool of knowledge from a lot of different minds. There may be a hundred different mathematicians and scientists pouring all of their accumulated thoughts and theories into my head, and if I can receive and handle all this and eventually grow to understand it, there will come a time when it will be *my* knowledge too."

"The way Lynda's painting is hers?" Sandy asked bitterly. "She's living in a world that doesn't even touch ours anymore."

"Well, Lynda's different," Ruth admitted. "She's kind of gone under."

"She's possessed," Sandy said.

"We have to escape." Kit made her voice firm. "There has to be a way —"

She broke off the sentence at the sound of voices in the hall.

Professor Farley appeared in the doorway. His crinkled old face was as friendly as ever, and his white hair and little pointed beard gave him the look of an underweight Santa.

"Nine-thirty," he said pleasantly. "It's time for you young ladies to be climbing the stairs to get your beauty sleep."

Glaring at him, Kit got to her feet.

"I don't need beauty sleep. All I need is to get out of here and go home. My stepfather is an attorney, did you know that? You just wait until he finds out I've been held here against my will. He'll have you put in jail."

"Now, Kit," the professor said, "we don't need that kind of talk. Your parents have placed you in our charge

131

for the semester, and it would be very lax of us indeed if we let you go charging off in all directions. You are our responsibility, both legally and morally."

"Morally," Kit growled. "You don't know the meaning of the word. What about all the letters we've written to our friends and families, the ones we've laid out on the hall table for you to mail for us in the village? You stole them, that's what! Do you call that 'moral'? It's not only wrong, it's against the law."

"Nobody has stolen anything," Professor Farley told her calmly. "Your letters are in a neat pile in Madame's office, and you may have them back anytime you so desire. And some of them did go out — the early ones in which there were no disturbing references to 'strange dreams' and 'odd things happening.' I'm sure your parents were delighted to receive them."

"One thing I've been wondering," Ruth said. "What happened to the other schools, the ones in Europe? Madame had two of them there. Why did they close down?"

"For various reasons," the professor told her, "none of which have anything to do with Blackwood."

"What about the girls in those schools?" Sandy asked. "What kinds of talents did they have? Did they compose music and write poetry?"

"Indeed, they did," Professor Farley said. "Many beautiful contributions to the culture of the world came forth from Madame Duret's previous students. I think I may go so far as to say that some of their creations were true masterpieces."

"Then where are they?" Kit asked him. "What was done with them? Why haven't we ever heard about them?" She paused as a thought occurred to her. "The Vermeer — the one Madame said she discovered at an auction! She didn't buy that painting at all! It was painted by one of the girls in her other schools! Madame got a fortune for it! She sold it as an original!"

"It was an original," Professor Farley said. "It was the work of Vermeer, no matter whose hand it was that held the brush."

"But couldn't experts tell the age of the painting?" Ruth asked in bewilderment. "The paint would be different and so would the canvas."

"You are forgetting," Professor Farley said, "that Madame is herself an expert on art. She supplied her students with used canvases of the proper vintage, scraped down to the original gesso. She was also able to supply paints made from lapis lazuli and cochineal. The final look of aging is not difficult to achieve. We baked the paintings in a hundred-degree oven for two hours and then rolled them to bring up the craquelure."

I won't go to sleep, Kit told herself. I may sit here all night, but I will not close my eyes.

It was a futile vow, and she knew it. Sleep waited behind her door like an all-encompassing fog. The moment she stepped into her room a heavy drowsiness would fall upon her, almost as though she had been administered a sleep-inducing drug, and her eyes would be falling closed before she reached the bed.

Tonight she fought it by crossing to the window. Pressing her forehead against the cold glass, she stared out into the night. At first she could see nothing but darkness. Then, as her eyes became adjusted, she saw the black shapes of the trees begin to emerge against the sky and realized that somewhere, too high to be seen from the house, there must be a full moon.

This is the wing, she thought, where the Brewers slept. Perhaps the Brewer babies were born here. This is where they had their nursery and where the parents had their big master bedroom.

Suddenly, there sprang into her mind a vivid picture of a woman, perhaps a little younger than her own mother, standing at this window just as Kit herself was doing now. The woman was plump and dreamy-eyed, and she loved her home — she loved to stand here and gaze out at the summer garden and the stretch of smooth, green lawn leading to the sparkling pond.

The world seemed to shift, the night lifted from Kit's eyes, and she could see before her the same scene that the woman saw — a lush garden abloom with flowers and a sunlit lawn on which three little boys were playing. A baby carriage was parked in the shade of an oak tree, and a white uniformed nurse wearing a sun hat was leaning over it to speak to the tiny occupant.

How lovely, Mrs. Brewer thought. How happy I am! What a beautiful, beautiful life this is!

Kit felt the glow of the woman's happiness sweep through her as though it were her own. Then, as quickly as it had come, the vision was gone. She was herself again, Kit Gordy, and it was November, and outside the night lay thick across the brown lawn.

Turning away, Kit went over and seated herself on the edge of the bed. Madame's words came back to her, "The vibrations still remain a part of the house." Somehow, in his desperate grief over the loss of his family, Mr. Brewer had managed to call them back to him, the gentle, sweet-faced wife, the romping children. He had closed his doors to the outside world and continued to live with his spirit family just as he would have if they had been with him in body.

It was too much to comprehend.

Sleep was pressing upon her now. Kit could feel the weight of it upon her eyelids.

I won't give in, she told herself vehemently. I won't!

Softly, at the edge of her mind, she heard the music, faint and far away, but ready to move closer, to close in upon her and take her over if her consciousness faded even slightly.

Go away, Kit cried silently, whoever you are — go away! You've had your time on earth! This is my time! *Mine!*

The bed was soft, tempting, drawing her backward. Her head touched the pillow and sank helplessly into its feathery depths. Above her the wine-colored canopy seemed to sway, dizzily, hypnotically, and in her ears the music grew louder. It was not just the sound of a piano this time, but strings, the high, sweet voices of violins, the richness of violas, the melodious ripples of a harp. And then there came a flute, shrill and true as the song of a bird.

"No," she wailed. "No!"

But her resistance was gone, and it had closed upon her, and she was a part of it, being carried along on the sweeping tide of sound.

"You must write it down," the dream man told her. How easily he came to her now, as though he belonged there, at home within the confines of her mind. "You must put this on paper. It is too great to lose."

"I can't," Kit replied. "I don't know how to write music."

"I will tell you. Get up from the bed. Here, take my hand — let me lead you over to the desk. Pick up a pencil."

"I don't have any music paper. You must know that."

"You do — you do. See!"

And she did. It was there, a music notebook with the staffs outlined in pale blue, awaiting her use. Someone had brought it and placed it in her room while she was down in the parlor. Madame? Jules? The same person who had come into her locked room on another occasion to remove Lynda's first portrait? Once the question would have seemed important, but now it did not matter. One or the other of them, it was all the same.

"I don't want to," Kit said. "I don't want to write down anything. You can't force me to do something that I don't want to do."

But even as she spoke, her hand was reaching for the pencil. Her fingers closed around it and she lifted it and drew the paper toward her.

"Kit!" Through the pounding of the music there broke a familiar voice, calling her name.

"What — who —" With a decisive wrench, Kit tore through the barrier between the two worlds.

It was Sandy who was standing in the doorway. She was dressed in pajamas, her hair was mussed from the pillow, and her freckles stood out in startling relief against her white skin.

"It's so cold in here," Sandy said, wrapping her arms around herself. "Is your window open? How can you sit there like that when it's like the inside of an ice —"

She did not finish her sentence. The pencil in Kit's hand flew from her grasp and broke with a loud snap in midair. As though fired from a gun, the pointed end shot straight across the room.

Sandy screamed and threw her hands up to cover her face.

In horror, Kit watched the stream of blood burst forth from her friend's forearm.

"Sandy!" she cried. "You're hurt!"

Slowly, the red-haired girl lowered her hands and stood, gazing in bewilderment at the thin shaft of wood protruding from her arm. Dazedly, she reached over with her other hand and drew it out.

"Here, sit down." Kit hurried over to her and, with an arm around her waist, drew her over to the desk chair. "I'll get a washcloth. We've got to stop that bleeding."

She went quickly into the bathroom and grabbed the cloth from the edge of the sink and ran cold water over it. Then she wrung it out and carried it back to the bedroom.

"Press this over the spot. No — I will — I can use both hands."

Sandy stared at her in disbelief. "Why did you do it?"

"Me? You think I did this?" Kit exclaimed, holding the cloth tightly against the injury.

"Well, didn't you? Somebody broke that pencil and threw it at me. If you didn't, who did? There's nobody else —" Her voice broke and understanding came into her eyes. "I'm sorry, Kit. Of course, you didn't. *He* was here, wasn't he? The one with the music?"

"Yes," Kit said. Her hand was shaking as she pressed it upon the washcloth. She felt sick.

"Why?" Sandy whispered. "What does he have against me?"

"It wasn't you," Kit said. "It would have been the same with anybody who had come in just then, who had broken his control. He had me, Sandy. I was going to write down his music for him. When you called out my name your voice came through to me, and I got away."

"Who was it?" Sandy spoke with a choking sob in her voice. "Schubert?"

"I don't think so. It's been a long time since it was Schubert. That is, if I can judge by the music. In the beginning it was lovely, but now it's different, wilder, more discordant. It doesn't *feel* like Schubert."

"It's the same with me," Sandy said. "That's why I came here tonight. I had to tell you. Ellis is gone."

"Gone?" Kit felt a sudden surge of hope. "You're free?"

"No. Oh, no. It's just that Ellis has been replaced. This new one — I don't see him, as I did Ellis, but he's there. I feel him come into my mind, and it's like smoke, thick and gray and dirty."

"Did he tell you who he was?"

"He doesn't tell me anything. He doesn't talk to me, he talks *through* me. He speaks some foreign language. I can't understand him."

"We should have guessed it," Kit said. "That there would be others. Ruth told us it was that way with her right from the beginning, with a whole host of people pouring their thoughts into her. I felt it myself the night I woke in the music room. It wasn't just one voice then but a lot of them, all bidding for me as though I were some sort of community possession."

"But why? I mean, why now, when at the start it was just one?"

"Maybe the road's wider open now, and they can get through."

"Then we can expect it to get worse? More and more of them, crowding into our minds, shoving our own thoughts out, until there's nothing of ourselves left?" Sandy was crying now, soft, hopeless crying which had nothing to do with her injured arm.

Kit lifted the cloth. The blood was stilled. Raising her head, she met the misery in her friend's face with that on her own.

"We've got to fight it," she said. "We can't let down. We can't let them take us over."

"But how can we help it? They're stronger than we are, especially with there being so many of them. They don't have to stop to sleep the way we do, they can keep at us constantly."

"Then we'll have to get out. We'll plan an escape. After all, there are four of us. That's against four of them, if you count Lola. It's even sides."

"You're counting Lynda as one of us. What good would she be? And Ruth — she's more on their side than ours. She likes what's happening." Sandy shook her head. "You're dreaming, Kit. There's no way. We'll never break out of here. Our only hope is Christmas. If we hold out till then, we'll go home for vacation. Our folks expect us. There's no way Madame can hold us here over the holidays."

"That's true," Kit said. "And Madame knows it, and that's what scares me worst of all. Because it doesn't seem to bother her. How can she accept the fact that we'll leave here and tell our parents and never come back again?"

The answer lay there between them in the stillness of the room, too dreadful to acknowledge.

"Don't say it," Sandy said, but Kit spoke the words anyway.

"By Christmas," she said softly, "it won't matter any longer. We won't have to be at Blackwood for them to get through to us. They're digging in deeper every day. By Christmas, they'll be part of us, the spirit people. They'll have such control that no matter where we go, no matter what we do for the rest of our lives, we'll belong to them."

Chapter 16

———————◆———————

Dear Tracy —

How strange, to be writing a letter which I know will never reach you. And yet I must; perhaps having you to talk to is what is keeping me sane.

The days go by. I don't even bother to keep track of them any longer; they're all the same. We don't have classes now — they stopped soon after that night when I woke in the music room and forced Madame to tell us the truth about Blackwood. After that, it became impossible. How could we keep going to classes, studying and learning regular everyday schoolwork, knowing that it was just a cover-up for something else? How could we sit at a desk and listen to Madame or Professor Farley lecturing about history and literature and languages, as though they were regular teachers, when we know now what they really are?

And Jules! How could I possibly sit at that piano and play rinky-dink beginners' pieces for Jules, who has heard me playing music that no one has ever heard before, my fingers moving in patterns that some musical genius has arranged for me? Out of everything, what I find hardest to accept is Jules, the fact that he is part of this. Imagine him sitting there in the music room, night after night, making tapes, while I sat on the piano bench in some kind of stupor, being ruled by a ghost! And I thought he liked me. I really did, Tracy — the way he looked at me, and the tone of his voice, and there was something in his eyes that night when I saw the figure in the mirror and started to scream. He came running up the stairs ahead of the others, and he put his arms around me and held me, and he *cared*. I could have sworn it.

How silly I was to think that when all I am to him is part of a weird and awful experiment.

Now that the classes are gone, so too is the pretending. Madame Duret and Professor Farley and Jules no longer sit with us in the dining room. We eat alone — Sandy and Ruth and I — when we eat at all. Most of the time we're not hungry, and when we are it's easier to go out to the kitchen and make a sandwich than to try to choke down the meals that Lola prepares. We spend as much time as we can outside, in the garden and by the pond, but the weather is so bad that the wind and chill soon drive us in again.

Lynda is lost to us completely. We never see her at all. I know she is painting, for every once in a while Professor Farley goes into her room and brings out the canvases and carries them down to Madame's office. What they do with them after that, I don't know. Will they sell them, I wonder, as they did the Vermeer? Is that how Madame managed to finance the purchase of Blackwood — with a brand new manuscript by Hemingway, a poem by Kipling, some music that only Chopin could have composed? Is she even now trying to market the newly discovered pieces by Schubert that Jules has on his tape?

If only I could get into that office to the telephone. I

have dialed your number so many times in my imagination that it is almost a part of me; I write it with my finger in the dust on the bureau top and I see now that I have scribbled it several times over in the margin of this letter. I could dial it in my sleep, I think, if I could reach the phone. But the office door is kept locked.

And Lynda's door also. They keep that locked so that we can't go in and "distract" her. Madame has the key, and she gives it to Lola to use when she brings up the trays. Sandy and I stand outside the room sometimes and try to talk to her, but Lynda doesn't answer. I feel that she might speak to Ruth. If anyone could get through to her, Ruth could — they have been friends for years — but Ruth won't call in to her. She says that the work Lynda is producing is too important to be slowed down by silly conversations.

We stay away from Ruth as much as possible, Sandy and I. Being with Ruth is almost as bad as being in the room with Madame Duret herself. Ruth isn't one of us anymore. She has accepted this thing, and she is riding with it like someone on top of a wave. Her eyes are shining with excitement, and she carries a notebook with her at all times so that she can write down the things that "come" to her. I looked into the notebook once, and it is like a strange code with numbers and signs and odd diagrams.

I won't accept it! Not as long as I'm alive, I won't! I will fight it all the way! I am going to get out of here, Tracy, somehow — some way — I *will* get out of here!"

Kit folded the letter, placed it in the pocket of her jeans, and left the room. She did not bother to lock her door, knowing now how senseless the formality was. She did not look in the mirror at the end of the hall. She did not want to know whom she might see there.

Descending the stairs, she went softly down the hall to Madame's office and tried the knob. It would not turn.

One time, she thought, *it will. She cannot keep it locked always. There will come a day when she forgets, and when she does, I will be in there so quickly that no one can stop me. It's just a matter of waiting and watching and trying.*

Beyond the office the door to the parlor stood open and there was a fire burning in the grate. Lola was in the room, dusting. Kit paused, but she did not enter. There was no use trying to talk with Lola. She did not know how much Lola understood of the situation at Blackwood, but whatever it might be, she would relate to no one but Madame Duret.

Kit continued down the hall until she reached the music room. From behind the closed door, she could hear the sound of the piano. She listened a moment and then, without knocking, opened the door.

Jules was seated on the piano bench, his back toward her, playing softly to himself. He stopped when the door opened and turned to see who had entered. This time he did not seem irritated by the intrusion.

He said, "Hi."

"Hi." Kit stood staring at him, wondering how she could ever have found him attractive. He looked like his mother, and she hated them both.

"What are you playing?" she asked him bitterly. "Something from Schubert?"

"Kit, please." He made a helpless gesture. "I don't want us to be enemies. I like you a lot. I have right from the beginning. I wish you'd try to understand my position."

"What, exactly, *is* your position?" Kit asked coldly.

"Well, it's not that of an accomplice in a crime. You're trying to make me feel guilty, and it's not fair. My mother has a gift, a marvelous one. She's given you a chance to help enrich the world. Why do you find that so upsetting?"

"Why do I find it upsetting!" Kit regarded him incredulously. "How would you feel if it were you, being used as a kind of vehicle for dead people! And since the subject's come up, why is it that you're not taking an active part in this experience? Isn't your mind 'young and clear and uncluttered' enough for your mother to want to use it?"

"Evidently not," Jules said stiffly, "or I'm sure she'd have made me a receiver also. Everybody isn't tuned for this sort of thing. You're one of the lucky ones."

"Stop saying that," Kit told him. "There's nothing lucky about it. Jules, I want to ask you something. The two other schools — the ones your mother had in England and in France — what happened to those? What became of the girls who went there? Why did your mother close those schools and come to the United States?"

"I don't know," Jules said. "I've never asked her."

"How can you not know? You were there, weren't you, when the decision was made?"

"No, I wasn't," Jules said. "I was away at the conservatory. I've told you that. The only time I spent at my mother's schools was during vacations, when they were closed. I didn't take much interest in her work. I didn't realize then the extent of what she was doing."

"You didn't know she was a medium?"

"I knew she had talents in that direction," Jules admitted, "but I didn't know she was using her students as subjects. And I had no idea she was doing something as exciting as bringing back the creative geniuses of the world. It wasn't until she closed her school in France and made arrangements to come to the United States that

144

she told me about that. She thought that it would make me want to come with her."

"And is it the way you thought it would be?" Kit asked him. "Are you happy about this, Jules — honestly? Can you look at what's happening to Lynda — to Sandy — to all of us, and think it's right?"

"Kit, you've got to adjust to this," Jules said. "I agree — you girls aren't in good shape. But it's your own fault. You're fighting this so hard that you've got yourselves physically and mentally exhausted. I don't like to see you looking like this, all white and thin and worn out, and I *do* worry about it. But the answer isn't with us, it's with you. If you'd just accept the situation and go along with it, I'm sure you'd be fine."

"You don't see! You don't understand!" Kit cried in frustration. The tears, which she had never used to shed, were welling in her eyes. "Jules, if you do like me — if you're really my friend — then help me! Help us all! Get us out of here!"

Jules shook his head. "I can't. You know that. It would ruin everything."

"Then if you won't do that, will you do something else for me? Will you find out what happened to the other girls, the ones who went to your mother's European schools? There are files on them in her office. She told me so herself."

"What would you learn from that?" Jules asked. "They're probably scattered all over the place by now."

"You could look and see, couldn't you? What harm would that do?"

Jules shook his head. "I can't go plowing through my mother's private files. I'll ask her though, if you want me to, and let you know what she says. Or you can ask her yourself."

"A lot of good that will do," Kit exploded.

The tears were so near the surface now that she knew that if she stayed a moment longer she would not be able to control them. Turning abruptly, she left the music room, slamming the door behind her, and went out again into the hall.

A cold burst of air met her, fresh and damp from the outdoors, and she saw that the great front door was standing open. A familiar figure stood beside it, adjusting the collar of her coat.

Kit gave a startled cry and stretched out her hands.

"Natalie!"

The figure turned, and Natalie Culler gave her a nod of acknowledgment. She completed buttoning the top of the coat and moved as though in preparation to step outside.

"Natalie — wait! Don't go!" Kit hurried over to her. "What are you doing here?"

"Collecting my money," Natalie said shortly. "When your lady fired me, she owed me two weeks' back pay. I was so mad at the time, I just walked out without remembering it, but that money was mine. I earned every penny of it, and I came back today to get it."

"How did you get here?" Kit asked excitedly.

"By car. How else? Think I'm going to walk up from the village?"

"And you were able to get in the gate?"

"I called ahead," Natalie said. "She sent Mr. Jules down to open it. I guess she knew I wasn't about to be put off any." She paused to stare at Kit, and the anger on her face faded slightly, to be replaced by concern. "If you don't mind me saying so, you look awful, miss. You been sick?"

"Yes," Kit said. "We're all sick. The whole place is sick! Natalie, take me with you!"

"With me? You mean to the village?"

"Anywhere! The village would be fine. Just someplace where I can get to a telephone and make a call. Please, Natalie!"

"It's cold out. You don't have a coat on."

"It doesn't matter! I won't be cold!"

"The missus would be furious," Natalie said uncertainly. "She'd likely have me arrested for kidnaping. Why don't you just write your folks and have them come for you, miss? That would be the best way to leave here, if that's what you want to do."

"I can't," Kit told her desperately. "Our letters are all —"

She broke off the sentence as she heard a door open into the hall behind her. There was a moment of silence.

Kit did not have to turn. She could tell from Natalie's expression whom it was that she would see.

"Natalie!" Madame Duret's voice was like ice. "You will please to be on your way. I have given you your wages, and I did not invite you to stay and visit."

"Yes, ma'am." There was a flash of pure hatred across Natalie's face. She turned defiantly to speak to Kit. "Good-bye, miss. You take care of yourself now. I hope you're feeling better soon."

"Wait — please!" Kit struggled to find words, and then, in a final frantic effort, she pulled the letter from her jeans pocket and thrust it quickly into Natalie's work-worn hand.

"Here," she whispered hurriedly, "take this and mail it."

Natalie glanced down at the wadded paper in bewilderment.

"Mail it? To who?"

"Tracy Rosenblum," Kit said. "She lives at —"

147

"Kathryn!" Madame spoke from directly behind her. "Come inside away from that open door. You will take a chill."

Natalie threw her one startled glance and stepped hurriedly out the door, pulling it closed behind her. She had the letter in her hand, but Kit could feel no thrill of triumph. There was no way possible that Natalie could mail it when it bore no address.

Chapter 17

———◆———

That night the winds came. Far and thin at first, like quarrelsome children arguing in the distance, and then closer, shrieking and crying in high, shrill voices in the branches of the trees outside the fence, they made their way to the doors of Blackwood and tried to get in.

All night long, they circled the house, trying the windows, howling around corners, wailing in the eaves, until when morning came Kit was certain she had not slept at all.

Then she realized that her right hand was cramped from writing and that the music book that lay on her desk was half filled.

"It's the same with me," Sandy told her later. "I try to fight it, but there's just so long you can hold out. I don't plan to sleep, and then suddenly it's morning, and I *have* slept."

Apologetically, she offered Kit a sheet of paper.

"Another poem?" Kit glanced at the paper and handed it back. "I can't read that. It's in French."

"I can't read it either. It's in my handwriting, though, so I know I wrote it down."

"Shall we get Ruth to translate?"

"I hate to ask her," Sandy said. "She'll enjoy doing it, and I don't want her to enjoy it. That sounds terrible, doesn't it?"

"Yes," Kit agreed. "Still, I know what you mean. She's taking such pleasure in this that I want to smack her." She paused and then said, "We don't have much choice. It's either ask Ruth or Madame or Jules, and Ruth's better than the others. You do want to know what you wrote, don't you?"

"I suppose," Sandy said, pocketing the paper. But she made no effort to go to find Ruth, and neither did Kit, who felt as drained and exhausted as though she had been out-of-doors all night, running with the winds.

They spent most of the day together in Sandy's room, reading, talking a little, and playing a half-hearted game of cards. Late in the afternoon the rain began, lightly at first and then with increased strength, so that by evening the gentle patter on the roof had become a dull roar. At six-thirty they went down to the dining room, not so much from hunger as from the realization that neither of them had eaten since the night before. It was Lola's evening off, and the meal left out on the table consisted of some withered-looking cold cuts and a bowl of soggy potato salad. The candles flickered erratically, and beyond the long windows an occasional flash of lightning streaked the black sky.

The food looked even less appetizing once they had put it on their plates than it had on the serving platter.

"I can't take it," Sandy said. "I'm sorry, I just can't make it go down."

"We've got to eat something," Kit told her. "We need all the strength we can get." But after one or two forced mouthfuls, she too shoved her plate away. A great roll of thunder filled the room, and the chandelier began to sway, moving slowly back and forth like an ornate pendulum, while the hundreds of tiny crystals caught the light from the candles and threw it in a strange, iridescent pattern upon the far wall. Outside the wind screamed and tree branches scratched at the windows like clutching hands.

"Let's go to the parlor," Kit said. "At least there'll be a fire."

Ruth was there ahead of them, leafing through her ever-present notebook and eating a peanut butter sandwich.

"I went out to the kitchen and made it myself," she said, cramming the last wedge into her mouth and swallowing. "I couldn't face that stuff on the table."

"That's a good idea. Maybe we'll do the same thing in a little while." Kit crossed the room to stand before the fire. The heat felt good against her back, and the crackling of the logs was the first cheerful sound she had heard in a long time.

"Why don't you give her the poem," she suggested to Sandy, "and see what she can make of it."

"Another offering from Ellis?" Ruth asked, closing her book.

"No," Sandy said. "It's in French. Ellis's poetry is all in English." She dug the paper out of her pocket and held it out.

Ruth took it and sat for a moment in silence, her eyes flicking from left to right as she scanned the lines.

"Cripes," she said softly, "you don't want me to read you this."

"Why not?"

"You just don't, that's all. It's — not like that other stuff you wrote."

"I don't care," Sandy said. "I want to hear it. I want to know what it is I've been writing."

"Well — okay." Ruth gave a slight grimace. "Just don't say I didn't warn you." She began to read, slowly, in an expressionless voice. As one word followed another, Kit, standing mesmerized in front of the fireplace, could not believe what she was hearing.

Sandy's face grew paler and paler. Finally she made a gesture to cut off the translation.

"No more. Don't read anymore."

"I told you," Ruth said. "I knew you wouldn't want to listen."

"It's sickening," Sandy said in a choking voice. "I've never used words like those in my life. It's just foul, the whole thing. It makes me want to throw up."

"Well, don't blame me for it," Ruth said. "All I did was read it, the way you asked me to. Who's the author, if you don't mind my asking?"

"I hate to think." Sandy turned wretchedly to Kit. "Can you imagine the sort of creepy, demented creature that would spill out garbage like that?" She shuddered. "I feel dirty just for having held the pen. I wish now I'd never —"

She broke off in midsentence as the room went white with a glare of brilliant light. Instantaneously there came a crash of thunder so tremendous that the ceiling seemed to lift with the impact and a picture on the wall by the window lurched from its nail and fell with a clatter to the floor. At the same moment, the electric lights flickered and went out.

In the sudden silence that followed, Kit could hear her heart pounding in rhythm with the drumming of the rain.

"That —" She tried to speak and found that her voice

had to be dragged from her throat. "That was a close one."

Ruth nodded. Her glasses caught the firelight and threw back a reflection of leaping flames. "I bet it hit the chimney."

"And now the lights are out. That's just great," Sandy said shakily. "Can you imagine climbing those stairs and trying to find our rooms in the dark?"

"I don't want to imagine it," Kit said. "I'm going to sleep right here. I'll flip you for the sofa." She meant the words to be light, but they didn't come out that way.

There was the sound of voices in the hall beyond the parlor door. Madame's, sharp and commanding. Professor Farley's. Jules's — raised in a question.

There came another roll of thunder, farther away this time, and the door opened.

"Girls?" the professor said. "Are you all right in here?"

"I guess so," Ruth said. "Do you know what happened?"

"We think it got that big tree outside the dining room window. Jules is going to look, and Madame has gone to the kitchen to hunt for candles. There should be a supply of them there for use on the table."

"At least we have a fireplace," Sandy said. "We can pretend we're at camp and toast marshmallows and tell ghost stories." There was a moment's silence, and then, as the full significance of what she had said came through to her, she began to laugh. It was a high, strange laugh, and once it started it would not be stopped; it poured forth, like carbonated liquid from a bottle that had been shaken and uncorked, gushing out, wild and uncontrolled.

"Stop it," Ruth told her.

But Sandy could not stop. She sat down on the hearth and stared at them out of wide, frightened eyes, and con-

153

tinued to laugh while tears streamed down her cheeks in fire-colored rivulets and the wind shrieked around the corners of the house, straining to be heard over the beat of the rain.

"Sandra? My dear girl." The professor came slowly across the room in his cramped, old-man's walk, grotesquely silhouetted against the glow of the firelight, and bent to gaze into Sandy's face. "Please, my child. You will have to get control of yourself."

"She can't," Ruth said. "She's hysterical."

"She certainly seems to be." The professor raised his head. "One of you girls, go fetch Madame Duret. She'll know how to handle this."

"In the dark?" Ruth objected. "The kitchen's all the way to the back of the house."

"I'll go," Kit said.

"In all this blackness? You'll get lost in the hall."

"No, I won't."

Silently, Kit cursed herself for the eagerness in her voice. How was it possible that they did not hear it and turn to her in suspicious amazement? But, no — they were both bending over Sandy. There was no one to see her, no one to stop her.

She stepped through the door and pushed it closed behind her and started down the hall full of darkness.

She was not afraid. For the first time in weeks, it seemed, there was no fear in her. She was moving purposefully and directly toward the thing that she was going to do. But, quickly, for there was little time. Any moment now Madame might emerge from one of the doors at the far end of the hall, her hands filled with candles.

Kit walked close to the wall, guiding herself with one hand, trying to gauge the distance she had come in comparison with that which she still had to go. She came to the door of the music room; her hand felt the frame, crossed the emptiness of the gaping doorway, found the wall on the far side. She began to count her steps — one, two, three, four — how many feet would it be from the music room door to the door of Madame Duret's office? She attempted to picture it in her mind, but the depth of the darkness around her blotted out all memory of the way the hall looked in the daylight.

Ten, eleven, twelve — had she come too far? Had she somehow missed the doorframe? Or, worse still, might she have lost direction entirely and be working her way toward the entrance to the dining room?

Dear Lord, I hope not, Kit thought. If I end up there, I'll never be able to get myself turned around and started back again.

Thirteen, fourteen — and she was upon it. The paneling of the wall gave way beneath her hand to the smooth, hard wood of the door. With a breath of relief, Kit felt along it, inch by careful inch. On their first trip across, her fingers missed the knob. On the second, they found it.

Offering a silent prayer, Kit closed her hand upon it and gave it a turn. It moved so easily that she almost fell forward as the door swung open into the room beyond.

And she was in the office. She knew it by the feel of the carpeting beneath her feet, by the faint smell of paint from Lynda's canvases, piled there for storage. Although she had been inside this room only once before, Kit could have described every inch of it, and she moved forward without hesitation in the direction of the desk.

Her outstretched hand touched the back of the desk chair. She reached past this and felt the flat, smooth surface of the desk top beneath her palm. She groped onward — over a pile of papers, a portable typewriter — to her goal.

The telephone.

She would not be able to see to dial, but that did not matter. The final digit in the circle would bring her the operator.

In one minute, she thought, just one more minute, I'll hear Tracy's voice. Or her mother's or father's. And I'll say, "This is Kit — Kit Gordy at Blackwood. Help! You've got to help me!"

Her hand was shaking as she lifted the receiver and her other hand felt for the dial. So great was her anticipation that she had already drawn in her breath to speak when she realized that there was no dial tone. Silent and dead, the receiver lay against her ear.

For a long moment she stood there, unmoving, willing it to life. Then, slowly, she lowered it and let it fall from her hand onto the desk.

The clatter was loud. It did not matter. Nothing mattered now.

"It was our one chance," Kit said softly. "Our one last chance."

Never would there be another night like this one, with so much confusion and excitement, with people rushing in different directions and the office door forgotten and unlocked. It was a one-time occurrence. By the time the phone line was repaired, the house would be back to normal and the office secure against invasion.

If I were Sandy, Kit thought miserably, I'd have hysterics. I'd stand here and shriek and laugh and bang my head against the wall. Or I'd cry. I think I could cry from now to eternity and never get done.

But being herself, she did neither. She simply stood there in the darkness, leaning upon the desk, waiting for the inevitable. Madame would return to the parlor with the candles, and as soon as Professor Farley realized that

Kit was not with her, someone would be dispatched to find her. And whoever it was would not have to think long to know where to come.

It was only a matter of minutes. The hall beyond the doorway grew lighter and she heard the footsteps approaching. Then suddenly a flashlight appeared, turned straight into her face.

Jules's voice said, "Kit! What the devil are you doing in here?"

The flashlight beam moved to the desk top and found the telephone, receiver off the hook. She could hear Jules draw in his breath.

"You made a call?"

"Of course." Kit tried to keep her voice steady. "I called the police. They're on their way up from the village now. You'd better tell your mother to get those gates open, Jules."

"Then why haven't you hung up?" Jules came into the room and reached across her to pick up the receiver from the desk. He held it to his ear for a moment, then replaced it on the hook.

"Good try," he said. His voice was oddly gentle. "The lines must be down. Come on, Kit. Let's get back to the others."

"I don't want to go back," Kit said. "I won't sit there in that room with your mother and the professor and make conversation and act as though they're normal people."

"Kit — please — I wish you wouldn't feel this way." He tried to put his arm around her shoulders, but Kit twisted free and stepped quickly around the desk chair so that it stood between them.

"Okay," Jules said stiffly. "If that's the way you want it, I'll take you to your room. You'll have to let me do that because you'll never find your way without a flashlight." He moved so that the beam of light made a pathway across the carpet and bounced against the opposite wall.

It flickered upward across a pile of canvases and stopped — focused upon one that stood propped against the side of the filing cabinet.

It was a moment before either of them could speak.

Then Jules said softly, "Oh, my God!"

Chapter 18

———————

"Who did it? Who painted that — thing? It can't have been Lynda."

"It was," Kit whispered. "Who else?"

She stared at the picture as though hypnotized, nauseated and heartsick, yet unable to tear her eyes away. The scene before her depicted a form of torture more horrible than anything she could ever have imagined. In the foreground, so real that it seemed to be bursting from the canvas, a woman's white face shrieked out at them, contorted into an expression of unbearable agony.

"But I thought —" Jules's voice was hoarse with shock, "I thought she was painting landscapes! Rivers, fields, pretty things —"

"Turn the light away."

Kit closed her eyes and when she opened them again the beam had dropped and the picture was coated with darkness.

"Now, do you see?" she asked quietly. "Do you begin to understand?"

"It's insane! Whoever created that is obscene — horrible!"

"It wasn't Thomas Cole."

"My God, no!" He sounded bewildered. "Who? Do you have any idea? Has she told you?"

"I haven't even seen her for weeks," Kit told him. "Your mother keeps her locked in her room upstairs. She won't speak to us when we call in to her through the door. Didn't you know?"

"I knew she spent most of her time in her room painting, but I thought —" Jules's voice broke. "Can you imagine, being in there alone, painting things like this? Holding a brush and watching them appear before you on canvas?"

"I can imagine it," Kit said, "and so can Sandy. Once the roads to the other world are opened, there's no controlling who travels along them. Can you see now why your mother didn't want to use you for a subject? You're her son. No mother would do this to her own son."

"My mother doesn't realize," Jules said uncertainly. "I'm sure she doesn't."

"She's seen the pictures. They're stored here, right in her office."

"Perhaps this is a new one. Professor Farley might have brought it down today."

"There's a pile of others. Do you want to look at them and see?"

Kit could not see his face, but she knew what must be on it by the sound of his voice.

"No."

"Jules," she said softly, "the other day, I asked you about what happened to the girls who went to your mother's European schools. You couldn't tell me. The files are here, right in that metal cabinet. All we have to do is open it and look."

"I couldn't," Jules said.

"You must! You owe us that!" Kit reached out in the darkness and touched his arm. "Please, Jules, we have to know! Don't you see, whatever it is that happened to them is what is destined to happen to us! Doesn't it matter to you? Don't you *care?*"

"Of course I care." He shifted the light to rest upon the cabinet, and in doing so it flicked across the side of the picture, catching once again the woman's tortured face. Every detail was so real that it seemed that the blood must surely have fallen to stain the carpet beneath it.

Kit swallowed hard against a wave of sickness that rose in her throat, threatening to choke her.

"Okay," Jules said shortly. "Let's look."

They moved together to the cabinet, Jules still holding the flashlight. There were two drawers, one above the other.

Kit dropped to her knees, seized the handle of the top drawer, and pulled it out. It came easily, disclosing a set of ledgers, bound in black leather. Behind these were several piles of canceled checks, held together by rubber bands, and a file of receipts.

Kit regarded them wryly.

"I wonder if there's a record here of what she got for the sale of the Vermeer."

"We'll look at the girls' files," Jules said. "I agreed to that, but not to plowing through the financial records. Shove that closed and pull out the lower drawer."

"All right." Begrudgingly, Kit pushed the drawer back into place and drew forth the one below it. This moved less freely and made a slight creaking sound, as though the grooves along the sides had begun to rust.

"This is it!" Kit exclaimed, feeling her heart begin to beat faster. "It's all names, arranged alphabetically. 'An-

derson, Cynthia,' 'Bonnette, Jeanne,' 'Darcy, Mary' —
there aren't very many of them."

"She kept the student number small in the other
schools," Jules said, "just as she has here. Where do you
want to start?"

"With the first in line, I guess." Kit reached for the
folder labeled "Anderson." "Shine the light on it, will
you? Oh, dear —" She caught her breath in disappointment. "It's in French!"

"Are you surprised? It's my mother's native language.
Mine, too, when it comes to that." Jules took the file
from her hand. "Here — let me read it."

"Aloud!" Kit said. A moment passed, and she said
again, "Aloud, Jules! Translate it for me!"

"Let me skim it first." Slowly Jules moved the flashlight beam down the page, pausing here and there as
though to reread certain passages. When he had finished
he replaced the file and drew out the next one.

"What did it say?" Kit demanded. "What happened
to Cynthia Anderson?"

"Stop pushing me, Kit," Jules said gruffly. "I want to
go through the rest of these. You can't tell anything by
one particular case."

"Well, hurry. Somebody might come looking for us
any minute." Kit bit down on her lip in frustration and
lapsed into silence. Outside the storm continued to howl.
In the office there was no sound except for the occasional
rustle of paper as Jules completed one history and reached
for the next.

After what seemed hours, he placed the final folder
back into the drawer and pushed it shut.

"Come on," he said. "We're going back to the parlor."

"Is that all you're going to say?" Kit's voice was squeaky
with rage. "You go through twenty sets of records, and

when you get finished you don't tell me one single thing?"

"I will tell you 'one single thing,' " Jules said. "That thing is that I'm getting you out of here."

"You're — *what?*" Kit stared across at him, trying to make out his face. "Did I hear you right? You're getting us *out?*"

"The sooner, the better," Jules said. "Now — tonight, if that's possible. If not tonight, then first thing in the morning."

"But, what did they say? What was in those files? You have to tell me!"

"I don't have to tell you anything." Jules got to his feet and reached down for her hand. "It doesn't matter what those papers said. What does matter is that you're getting what you want. You're going home, you and the rest of them, if it means I have to drive you there myself."

There was such determination in his voice that Kit did not push the question further. She let him pull her to her feet and, shining the light ahead of them, lead her out of the office and back along the downstairs hall. The glow from the fireplace was a rosy strip under the parlor door.

Jules pulled the door open and, still holding Kit's hand, drew her with him into the room. Glancing quickly about her, Kit saw that the scene had not changed measurably from the one she had left half an hour before. Sandy was still seated on the hearth, but she was quiet now, bent forward with her face buried in her hands, and Professor Farley stood above her, talking to her soothingly. Ruth had shoved a chair over by the fireplace and was trying to read in the flickering light.

Madame Duret stood with her back to the doorway, placing a set of candleholders on the mantel. She turned as she heard the door open and said, "Jules? Where did you find her?"

His voice was low. "She was in the office, just as you suspected, trying to make a phone call. The line must be down, though. The phone was dead."

"Thank goodness for that." Madame turned her icy gaze upon Kit. "Did you really imagine you would accomplish something by that sort of maneuver? I should think by now, Kathryn, that you would have become adjusted to the fact that you are going to remain at Blackwood until you are sent home for the holidays. Nothing you do will change this, and life will become much simpler for you and for the rest of us if you will accept the situation for what it is."

"I don't have to accept it!" Kit cried defiantly. "None of us do! Jules is taking us out of here!"

"That's ridiculous," Madame said firmly. "Jules is doing nothing of the sort. That is something he told you to keep you from making a scene. Jules despises unpleasantness."

"It wasn't!" Kit told her. "He means it! He promised!" She clutched tightly at the strong hand that held hers. "You did promise, Jules — you were telling the truth?"

"Yes," Jules said.

The word fell into the room like a stone into a pond. One single word, but in the silence that followed ripple after ripple rose and went sliding across to splash against the walls. Ruth lowered her book to stare at him unbelievingly. Sandy lifted her face from her hands. Professor Farley turned, his mouth falling open.

Madame Duret stood frozen, a candle in each hand.

"What did you say?" she asked her son.

"I said 'yes.' I am taking them out of here. Tonight, if the storm lets up." Jules spoke quietly. "I read the files, Mother."

"The files?"

164

"From the cabinet in the office. The ones you kept on the girls from the European schools. I read the records on all of them, the things they did, the things that happened to them."

"Then how is it that you can speak of letting our Blackwood girls go now?" Madame was incredulous. "You saw their accomplishments? That one little Jeanne Bonnette wrote three entire novels. We had them published under a nom de plume and the royalties made possible the purchase of Blackwood. And the black girl from Marseille — what was her name, Gigi? Over fifty oils, straight from the period of the French Impressionists."

"I saw Lynda Hannah's latest oil," Jules said.

"Oh? Well, she is going through a stage. We cannot sell *that*." Madame gave a sigh of regret. "I fear that Lynda's productivity may be reaching its end. But as for the rest of them, they are only beginning! The good months lie still ahead! Who knows what may come forth from them!"

"You think that's important?" Jules asked.

"And *you* do not? That I cannot believe. I heard you yesterday myself, playing over Kathryn's last tape."

"That was yesterday — before I knew." He regarded his mother with amazement. "Do you really think I'd want to go on with it, having read those reports? How can *you* want to?" Jules was fighting to control his voice. "Mother, don't you understand? I know what happened to those girls!"

"What did the reports say?" Kit begged. "Please, Jules — she's not going to give in. You have to tell us."

Jules hesitated, then made his decision.

"Out of the twenty, four of them are dead."

"Dead!" Kit whispered.

"Three committed suicide. One fell, trying to climb

165

out of a third-story window at the school. That was classified as an accident."

"And — the others?" Kit could hardly bring out the question.

"The others went insane. *Every single one of them is now in a mental institution*."

From her place on the hearth, Sandy gave a little moan.

Professor Farley shook his head reprovingly. "That was a very unwise statement to make in front of these girls, Jules. It can do nothing but upset them and make them unhappy. It was a cruel thing to tell them."

"Cruel!" Kit cried. "You can call Jules 'cruel'? You, who knew it all along! You and Madame Duret, the two of you — you're not even human! You're like two great big black vultures, feeding on our brains!" She turned frantically to Jules. "Let's leave now! It doesn't matter about the storm. I'd rather get hit by a falling tree or washed off the road or *anything* than spend one more night in this awful place!"

"I'm with you," Sandy cried, pulling herself to her feet. "Ruth?"

"You're darned right, I'm with you," Ruth said. Her face was dark with anger. "This is one little piece of news nobody bothered to tell us. It's one thing to be a receiver — I could go that route fine — but it's something else entirely to know it's going to destroy you."

"Now, girls, calm yourselves," Madame commanded. "Jules, I am furious with you for causing this disruption. Perhaps there was some instability among our past students. We had not perfected our entrance tests at that point and inadvertently selected some emotional types who were too high-strung to be able to adjust to the situation. This has no bearing whatsoever upon what will

166

happen at Blackwood. Each individual is different; you know that."

"Twenty out of twenty is good enough odds for me," Ruth said. She was on her feet now, clutching her notebook against her chest. "If I'm lucky enough to be that one-in-a-million case who pulls through nicely, I don't plan to stick around to find out about it. You were right all along, Kit. I'm ready to go."

"Kit, you go get Lynda," Jules said. "Mother, we'll need the key to her room and the one to the gate. How long will it take you girls to pack?"

"Hardly any time at all," Kit told him. "I'm willing to leave everything I came with except my father's picture, and it'll just take a minute to get that."

"I don't need anything," Sandy said. "I just want to get into that car. We can find out the bus schedule when we get to the village."

"I am afraid you're forgetting something," Madame Duret said quietly. "And that is that the keys are not at your disposal."

"You have them," Jules said.

"Of course I have them, but I do not for a moment intend to give them to you, nor do I plan to tell you where they are. The lock on the front gate will stay locked, and you will remain here, every one of you."

"You can't hold us here!" Kit cried. "Jules won't let you!"

"Jules cannot do very much about it. It distresses me to see him take this unreasonable and sentimental attitude, but young men are inclined to get romantic notions. In this case, I am sure common sense will eventually win out. Jules is an intelligent boy, and the advancement of music is very important to him."

"Not this important," Jules said. "Not when lives and

sanity are at stake. Mother, I can't believe this. Where is your sense of values?"

"Your mother's value system is a good deal more solid than yours, young man," the professor said irritably. "I should hope you would show some respect for her knowledge and experience. If nothing comes from this experiment but one short poem by one of the immortal poets of history, it will be worth more than the lives of four commonplace youngsters."

And there was a time, Kit thought in amazement, when I thought that old man was *sweet!* Anger was building in her to such a point that she was ready to explode with it.

"There's one thing *you've* forgotten," she said to Madame Duret, fighting to keep her voice steady. "That is that we are the ones who receive the material from the world beyond. It's ours — it comes through us — and it doesn't have to go one step farther."

"If that is some kind of threat —" Madame Duret began.

"It isn't a threat, it is a statement of fact." Kit lifted her chin defiantly. "There's no way in the world you're going to get this material if we don't want you to. Do you know what I'm going to do the next time I find myself writing down music? I'm going to tear the paper up into tiny pieces and flush them down the john."

"You would not dare!" Madame's eyes were blazing.

"I would! Just wait and see!"

"And so would I." There was a note of renewed courage in Sandy's voice. "You'll never get another poem of mine, starting with this one!"

Before anyone realized what she was about to do, she pulled a wadded paper from her sweater pocket and threw it into the fire.

The flames leapt high for a moment and there came a

low groan that seemed to rise from all corners of the room at once.

"Was that the one I translated for you?" Ruth asked.

"Yes, and that is just where it belongs — burned to ashes." Sandy made a grimace of disgust. "Horrid thing. I feel cleaner already having gotten rid of it."

"Stop them!" the professor cried. "We can't let them do this! What they're destroying is irreplaceable!"

"They will *not* do it," Madame's voice was a low hiss. "We will simply have to watch them, every minute of every day. We will chain them if necessary and stand over them and remove things from their hands the moment they are completed. We will not be defeated! The stakes are too high! The work is too important!" She turned to Ruth. "Hand me that notebook immediately."

"Go and get it!" Ruth cried.

Ripping the cover from the book, she lunged forward and hurled the pages into the fireplace. Instantly, the edges turned black and began to curl inward.

Madame gave a cry of rage and grabbed for the fire tongs, but Jules moved in to block her.

"It's too late, Mother, can't you see that? The experiment's blown up in your face. This set of girls isn't going to give in. Let them go, let me take them out of here. Holding them isn't going to accomplish anything. It's just not going to work."

The pages from Ruth's notebook burst into a crackling blaze, and from its depths there came a shriek of such agonized fury that it shook the walls. The voice lifted in a scream, and another voice joined it and another, until the room was filled with a chorus of hate-filled wails.

Suddenly, as though lifted by an unseen hand, the burning pages rose from the fireplace and flew straight out into the room in a shower of flaming segments.

Kit instinctively threw up her arms to protect her face

as the deadly missiles whizzed past, and she gave a cry of pain as one brushed her arm. All about her she could hear gasps and cries, and when she lowered her hands she saw to her horror that the draperies over the windows were on fire. The great orange flames gobbled greedily at the rich material and in a moment's time they had spread to the sofa and the overstuffed chair.

"Now, see what you have done! You wretched girls — you have angered them past endurance!" Madame started across the room. "I will call the fire department."

"You can't do that!" Jules flung out an arm to stop her. "The phone's out, remember? Our one chance is to drive to the village for help. Give me the gate key!"

"I know what you intend! You will take the girls with you!"

"Sure, I will," Jules said. "But you don't have a choice. Mother, for God's sake, this old house is an absolute fire-trap! It's ancient, the wood is dry — there's nothing to stop it!"

"Oh — damn you! Damn all of you!" Madame glared at them helplessly. Then with a jerk of her hand she reached into her skirt pocket and pulled out a ring of keys. "Here — it is the big, square one. Hurry, Jules! Hurry! If they do not come quickly it will be too late."

"I'll make it as fast as I can," Jules told her. "Now, come on, let's get out of here!"

He threw open the parlor door and led the way through the dark hallway to the front door. A moment later they were outside with the wind wild against their faces and the icy rain full upon them.

"We'll go to my apartment," Professor Farley called, starting across the lawn. "That's detached from the house. Unless the wind changes, we'll be all right there."

Madame's black figure fell into step behind him, and

Jules caught Kit's arm and shoved her toward the driveway.

"You and the other girls wait out there. I'm going to get the car."

"We're leaving!" Sandy was half laughing, half crying. "Can you believe it, Kit, we're actually leaving! By morning we'll be on our way home and we'll look back on Blackwood and the whole thing will seem like a bad dream!"

"I'll call my parents from the village," Ruth said. "They'll wire me plane fare. I can bus to the nearest town that has an airport."

"Home," Kit said. "It sounds like heaven."

And then her heart caught in her chest. She turned and stared back at the house behind them with the flames bright behind the lower windows, and as she watched, she saw a malicious red tongue of fire appear suddenly at the second-floor level, licking up the edge of a bedroom window.

"Sandy! Ruth!" Horror filled her voice. "We're forgetting — *there's Lynda!*"

Chapter 19

———◆———

"Lynda!" Sandy repeated the name, stunned. "Oh my God! In all the excitement, we forgot about her."

"You wait here," Kit told her, "and tell Jules where we've gone. Ruth and I will go get her."

"Speak for yourself," Ruth said shortly. "I don't plan to commit suicide. Do you see how that fire has spread already? Lynda's room is around on the side, almost directly over the parlor."

"You don't mean we should leave her there!" Kit exclaimed incredulously. "She'll be burned alive!"

"And what do you think will happen to us if we go back into that place to get her?" Ruth shook her head. "I'm sorry. It's tragic, but there's nothing we can do. Perhaps when the fire department gets here —"

"In an hour?" Kit cried. "It will be that by the time we drive the distance to the village and they round up their volunteers and get back here. By that time the place will be ashes!"

"Well, I'm not planning on being ashes with it," Ruth said. "Face it, Kit, the fire's spread all across the front of the house. Look at those windows — they're aglow with it! We'd never even get in the front door."

"We can go through the kitchen," Kit said. "There hasn't been time for it to have got that far. Ruth, think — this is Lynda, your best friend!"

"I'm sorry," Ruth said again. "I honestly am. It's just that there's no chance in the world of our getting up to that second floor and back down again. We wouldn't be saving Lynda, we'd be throwing our own lives away for nothing."

"I'm afraid she's right, Kit," Sandy said shakily. "Our best bet would be to get under Lynda's window and yell up to her. Perhaps we could get her to jump."

"She'd never hear us through the noise of the storm."

"We could throw stones up against the glass."

"Do you really think she'd react to that when she won't even answer us when we call through the door?"

"It's a chance, isn't it?" Ruth said. "It's better than nothing."

"Not *much* better than nothing," Kit retorted. "You can go throw stones if you want to. I'm going to try to get inside through the kitchen."

"You mustn't! You'll get trapped in there!" Sandy grabbed for her arm.

Kit shook her off impatiently.

"I'm not going to let Lynda die up there if there's any possible way to get her out!"

Leaving the other girls behind her, she started on a run around the side of the house. As she rounded the corner the wind struck her full force, whipping the raindrops against her as though they were pellets of steel. Somewhere to her left lay the pond, but she could not see it for the darkness and the driving sheet of rain. Her feet found the familiar gravel path, as dried stalks from the long dead garden raked her ankles and a rosebush threw out a thorny arm to slash her cheek.

"Kit! Wait!" Sandy's voice echoed behind her, thin and far.

I can't wait, Kit called back silently. There's no time to wait!

At the back of the house her way was easier for the planting was less dense and the eaves offered some protection from the rain. She floundered on through the heavy blackness, ran against the incinerator, reversed herself, and found the path that led to the kitchen door. For one panicky instant she was afraid that it might be locked, but it opened easily, and a moment later she was inside, groping her way through the dark kitchen.

She reached the far side, shoved open the door into the dining room, and staggered back, choking, under a great rush of acrid smoke. Letting the door swing closed again, she leaned weakly against the edge of the counter, gasping for breath and wiping the stinging fumes from her eyes.

She would have to mask her face, but how, in the darkness? Frantically she tried to recall the exact layout of the kitchen. There was a drying rack by the sink where Natalie used to hang the dish towels, but did Lola use it now that Natalie was gone?

Working her way back along the counter, Kit kept one arm outstretched, even with the wall. Her hand moved across the smooth tile — found the sink, the faucets, felt the soft touch of cotton cloth.

"Thank heaven," Kit breathed as her fingers closed over the towel and pulled it from the rack. She felt for the faucet and turned it on. The water ran cold, and when the towel was drenched she covered her head with it, letting the front fall forward over her face like a veil, and returned to the dining room door.

Now, when she opened it, she could face the smoke,

at least long enough to reach the stairway. It was not until she was halfway across the room that she realized that she was no longer walking blind. The faint glow of light from the hall beyond should have prepared her for what she would see there, but it didn't. Emerging from the dining room, she felt the heat strike her in one great blast. At the far end of the hall, the wall that had once enclosed the parlor was a solid panel of fire.

The hall was thick with smoke, but through it she could make out the curve of the stair leading to the second floor. She reached the first step and began her ascent, only to stop at the landing, horrified, as a second wall of flame leapt wildly in front of her.

"But it can't be!" she gasped, and then in shaken relief realized that this was only the mirror playing yet another of its devious tricks on her, catching and throwing back the image of the hall below in a blazing reflection.

Continuing her way forward, she reached the second-floor hall. Here it was cooler than on the lower level and the smoke was thinner; the only light was the reflection from the mirror, wavering and pale, but it was enough for her to see her way to Lynda's door.

She reached for the knob, twisted it, and gave a cry of frustration. How could she have forgotten that this door would be locked? There was no way to open it. By the time she could reach the carriage house to get the key from Madame she would not be able to return through the downstairs hall.

Making a fist, she began to pound upon the door.

"Lynda?" she shouted. "Lynda, are you awake in there? Do you hear me, Lynda?"

There was no sound from the room within. Kit pounded more loudly.

"Lynda, answer me! I know you're in there — you have

to be. Lynda, there's a fire! Blackwood is on fire! Do you hear?"

Was it her imagination or was there a faint rustling sound, a movement, a gasp of understanding? Kit began to kick, crashing her foot time and again upon the wood of the lower panel.

"Blackwood is on fire! Blackwood is burning!"

"Who —" The voice on the far side of the door was small and tentative, half dazed as though the speaker were just waking from sleep. "Who — is that?"

"It's Kit! Kit Gordy!" Kit ceased her pounding and brought her face down to the level of the keyhole. "Lynda, listen — you have to get out of there! The door's locked and I don't have the key to open it. The only way is by the window. You'll have to drop from the window."

"From the window?" Lynda echoed blankly. "But I can't do that. It's too high."

"Ruth and Sandy are standing down below," Kit told her. "They'll break your fall. Besides, it's lawn beneath you, not the driveway. You'll have to do it, Lynda, you don't have a choice. There's no other way."

"But, my paintings!" Lynda exclaimed. "I can't leave them!"

"You'll paint new ones." The statement was flatly untrue, but she felt no guilt in uttering it. "Don't waste time talking, get over to the window. Go on, now! I'll stay here until I know you're all right. Go look — are the girls down there?"

There was a moment of silence. When Lynda's voice came again it was faint with increased distance.

"Yes, they're there — Sandy and Ruth — and Jules. Jules is there with them."

"Open the window!" Kit called. "Hurry, get your legs over the sill! If you can lower yourself from the ledge you won't have as far to drop."

"It's raining," Lynda said wonderingly. "I didn't know it was raining. I can see them down there under the window. They're waving and holding their arms up to me. How is it I can see them when it's night?"

"It's the firelight shining from the windows!" The smoke in the hall was getting heavier and the cloth across her face had dried. "Jump!" Kit cried. "Please, Lynda, get on with it! I can't stay here much longer!"

There was no answer. Had the girl done it, or was she standing still by the window, staring down at the firelit figures awaiting her below? Kit rattled the knob.

"Lynda?" she called again.

There was no sound from within. Blackwood lay silent except for a steady crackling noise which, Kit realized suddenly, she had been hearing, half consciously, for some time. She drew a breath and began to cough uncontrollably. The soles of her feet felt hot. Bending, she pressed her hand against the hard wood floor and snatched it away again as quickly as though she had laid it against a hot griddle.

She could wait no longer.

"Good luck!" she called to Lynda, hoping the girl was not there to hear her, and, turning, she started back along the hallway to the stairs.

The hall seemed brighter now and the heat more intense, and in the mirror she could see herself emerging from the darkness like some grotesque apparition, with her rain-dampened clothes molded to her body and the dish towel draped across her head. She reached the top of the staircase, and as she gazed down a low moan escaped her.

"There's no way," Kit whispered. "No way."

Ruth had been right about the impossibility of this mission. In attempting to rescue Lynda, she had sacrificed herself. This stair was the only way down from the second floor, and the fire in the hall below had spread almost to its base.

Then this is how it ends, Kit thought, and somewhere at the edge of her mind she heard someone laughing, a malicious chortle that began softly and rose in a howling frenzy.

"Too good for us, were you!" the dream man cried. "Too good to waste your precious life recording our music! And now, what use will that dear life be to you?"

"It's my own!" Kit shouted back to him, finding strength in defiance. "At least it's my own life, right to the end!" She began to cough again and, half blind with smoke, she pressed her arm across her eyes, feeling the bravado fall away in the horror of reality.

"Mother!" she murmured helplessly. "Daddy, help me! What am I to do now?"

The habit of years, to call upon those two names. A hundred scenes rose from memory to flash upon the screen of her mind — her parents, strong, sure, arms outstretched to her, hands open to catch her own, eyes warm with concern, faces gentle with love. Her mother, regarding her worriedly — "Kit, dear, you will be happy here at Blackwood, won't you? I'd never enjoy a moment of our trip if I thought you weren't." Her father in that strange final visit, standing silent by her bed, gazing down at her —

"Kit, open your eyes."

The voice was low and steady, a never-to-be-forgotten voice, gruff with affection.

"You'll never get out of this place with your head in your arms."

I'm dreaming, Kit thought, and yet she knew that she wasn't. Slowly she raised her head and opened her eyes and stared up into the square, strong-featured face so much like her own.

"Dad!" Kit said softly. "Dad — it's you?"

For an instant longer the vision held, so real that she might almost have reached out and laid her hand against the sun-browned cheek. Then it blurred and was lost as hot tears flooded her eyes.

I'm so glad you're here! I won't be so afraid with you here with me. I should have known you'd come — that you wouldn't let me die alone.

She did not speak the words aloud, but she did not need to. She could feel her father's presence so strongly that he was almost a part of her. When his voice answered it came not from the hall before her but from somewhere within the depths of her own mind —

You are not going to die!

But there's no way out, Kit began — the fire — it's everywhere! No one could make it through that hall —

You must try.

Firm words, spoken in a tone that allowed for no argument. A command that must be obeyed. Kit found herself responding as she had as a child to these words, to his voice —

All right. All right, Dad — I'll try.

She descended the stairs. Later she would try to remember the way it had been, the slow step-by-step progress with the acrid smoke filling her lungs and the walls of Blackwood rising above her to the great arched ceiling, but the memories would not hold true. They would come in fragments. The trip down the stairs. The blazing hallway. The smoldering pit that had once been the parlor. The pressure upon her head —

Bend down. Get as low as you can — the air will be better.

The dining room where the chandelier swung madly above a flaming table, throwing back a million orange lights.

Again — the kitchen.

You must go to the gate. Do not stop for anyone. Go straight to the gate, and when you reach it, the Rosenblums will be waiting.

"The Rosenblums? But, how —"

The letter, she thought. Of course. I had the Rosenblums' phone number scribbled along the margins. Natalie must have read it and realized what the number meant and called them.

She believed him as she had always believed him, and she felt his hand guide hers to the knob of the kitchen door.

She did not remember later, stepping through it. She knew only that suddenly she was outside, running down the driveway, with the silly towel still upon her head and the rain in her face and the wind whipping cold against her shoulders. Ahead of her lay the iron fence and beyond that the black arms of trees waving wild against the sky. She could not see them for the darkness, but she knew that they were there.

Halfway down the drive she stopped and turned to look back at the house. There it stood, as it would stand forever in her nightmares, the great peaked roof outlined in flashes against the lightning-ruptured clouds. It had been from almost exactly this point that she had first glimpsed Blackwood, gray stone upon gray stone like a child's jigsaw puzzle, the windows ablaze in the late afternoon sun as though the interior were alive with flames.

"Can't you feel it?" she had said then to her mother. "There's something about the place — something —"

She knew the answer now.

Kit did not wait to watch the building fall. She turned

and began to run again into the clean, cold strength of the wind.

"Here I am!" she cried. "Here I am!" as headlights came round the curve in the road ahead and drew to a stop against the gate.